T0244979

Life
Expectancy

Life Expectancy

Alison Hughes

DCB

Canadian Heritage Patrimoine canadien   Canada Council for the Arts Conseil des arts du Canada

 ONTARIO CREATES | ONTARIO CRÉATIF  ONTARIO ARTS COUNCIL CONSEIL DES ARTS DE L'ONTARIO an Ontario government agency un organisme du gouvernement de l'Ontario Ontario

We acknowledge financial support for our publishing activities: the
Government of Canada, through the Canada Book Fund and The Canada Council
for the Arts; the Government of Ontario, through the Ontario Arts Council, Ontario
Creates, and the Ontario Book Publishing Tax Credit. We acknowledge additional
funding provided by the Government of Ontario and the Ontario Arts Council to
address the adverse effects of the novel coronavirus pandemic.

Library and Archives Canada Cataloguing in Publication

Title: Life expectancy / Alison Hughes.
Names: Hughes, Alison, 1966- author.
Identifiers: Canadiana (print) 20230198686 | Canadiana (ebook) 20230198694 | ISBN
9781770867093 (softcover) | ISBN 9781770867109 (HTML)
Subjects: LCGFT: Novels.
Classification: LCC PS8615.U3165 L54 2023 | DDC jC813/.6—dc23

United States Library of Congress Control Number: 2023934886

Cover art: Jennifer Rabby
Cover and interior text design: Marijke Friesen
Manufactured by Friesens in Altona, Manitoba in July, 2023.

 MIX Paper from responsible sources FSC www.fsc.org FSC® C016245

Printed using paper from a responsible and sustainable resource,
including a mix of virgin fibres and recycled materials.
Printed and bound in Canada.

DCB Young Readers
An imprint of Cormorant Books Inc.
260 Ishpadinaa (Spadina) Avenue, Suite 502, Tkaronto (Toronto), ON M5T 2E4
www.dcbyoungreaders.com
www.cormorantbooks.com

For M

After

THE OLD CLOCK ON HER bedside table read 2:25 a.m. Its ticking filled the room and bounced off the walls.

Chick, chick, chick …

Sophie listened to it biting off the seconds like a metronome, her shallow breathing keeping time. Staring up into the darkness, watching the deeper shadows of trees dance on her ceiling, she felt another uprush of raw panic. She thrashed out of bed and lunged for the light. From his cat bed, Nickleby lifted his shaggy head and gave her a long, baleful, yellow-eyed stare.

"Sorry," she said, sinking down, curling around him, stroking his thick black fur. He suffered it for a minute, then stalked away to clean off the affection.

This is why people get therapy *dogs*, she thought.

She sat on the floor with her back to the bed and stared at the wall, beyond the wall, beyond the house. The cold she felt had nothing to do with the temperature; she was numb-cold, bone-cold, dread-cold.

Chick, chick, chick …

She roused herself, looked around blankly, then skimmed a shaky finger down the pile of novels by her bed. Not one of them was interesting, none of them even possibly diverting. For the first time in her life, books failed her. They'd always been a solace, an escape. Not now. Maybe not ever again.

Her eye fell on a book she didn't recognize. *Good stuff, must read!* said her mother's purple ink on a Post-it Note. It was that book of plays she taught her undergraduates, the one Sophie had said she wasn't interested in. Sophie flipped the book open and stopped five words in at the stage directions for the first play.

A country road. A tree. How could the most benign, simple setting imaginable open up a sinkhole of dread?

A lonely house. A girl.

Sixteen years old and the curtain was already rising on the final act of her play. Nobody had prepared her for that. Nobody ever said, "Look out, Sophie, this play of yours might have a bitch of a twist! It might also be way, *way* shorter than you thought." Sophie imagined herself tussling frantically with an unexpected curtainfall.

If she had been asked, she probably would have imagined her life as a meandering path to a peaceful death at ninety; an unrecognizable Sophie, ancient and kindly and wise in a wooly shawl, soft, thinning white hair skimming a pink scalp, surrounded by loving children, grandchildren, and great-grandchildren. A perfect, old lady movie-death.

And yet here she was, alone, center stage, her script yanked away, forced to improvise because all the rules had changed.

What were the rules now? Where was her script?

She tossed the book of plays aside. She needed something short, light. She dug under her bed for a fashion magazine, grabbing randomly at the guilty stash. Officially, she despised the fashion industry. Flipping pages quickly, urgently, through a ton of ads, makeup tips, celebrity beauty secrets, flatter abs. All of it utterly meaningless. She felt old.

Chick, chick, chick …

Her flipping slowed; her hands stilled.

She stared down at the random advertisement that was face up. Pore cleanser, 4x the deep-cleaning action of soap, stop acne before it begins! A model with never-acned skin on one side, and on the other, a simplistic diagram showing epidermis, pore cavity, and the sinister, sludgy oil deposits. All the bad stuff hidden underneath the surface …

Just like me.

Stop it. Just stop …

She hunted unsuccessfully for a nail left to bite, then gnawed on the skin by her stubby thumbnail. She tasted metallic blood; *her* bad stuff hidden beneath the surface. Shouldn't her blood taste different now that she knew what was in it?

2:40 a.m. Nickleby wasn't even finished his cat bath. She wondered how she was ever going to get through this night.

Almanacs! Why hadn't she thought of the almanacs? Even as a kid she'd found facts and figures weirdly soothing, and for the last few years, running through a mental map of world capitals had been her go-to anti-insomnia strategy.

She stumbled on stiff legs over to her bookshelf and pulled out the most recent *World Almanac and Book of Facts* from the row of almanacs dating back to 2008. Ordered, structured information, rows of numbers, columns of data blocked symmetrically. Any subject you could think of: State Maps, Flags of the World, International Time Zones, Country Music Singers, the Electoral College, U.S. Unemployment by Industry, Boxing Champions

Alison Hughes

by Class, World History, Common Infectious Diseases, Selected Characteristics of the Sun and Planets. All the answers to everything in one thick paperback, a bargain at fifteen bucks.

She flipped past Veterans and National Parks, pausing briefly at Sexual Activity of U.S. High School Students (you couldn't trust that one; kids lie), then galloped through the book, flipping whole inches, a hundred pages at a time. Past Notable Islands, Student Loan Debt by State, Buildings, Bridges and Tunnels. She finally settled with relief on Nations of the World. Statistics, numbers, pure calming facts.

First up: Afghanistan. She skimmed down the country summary, past People, Geography, Government, Economy, Finance, Transport, and Communications. Her glance sharpened at Health. *Why is Health last? Pretty bloody important.* But it was the first subheading that had her sitting back.

Life expectancy: 49.9 male; 52.7 female.

Sophie stared down at the numbers.

Less than fifty years for men; that would be Dad. Fifty-two years for women; that's Mom. They'd be dead and gone tomorrow, tonight, like all the people their age in Afghanistan. That would be the end of their country road.

She couldn't get out of Afghanistan fast enough, crumpling the page as she flipped it. Longer lives in Albania (75.7 male, 81.2 female), but as she skittered through the A's, Angola plummeted: 54.8 male, 57.2 female.

She flipped obsessively, country to country, the standardized format drawing her eyes down to Health. To Life Expectancy.

Belize: 67.2 male, 70.4 female.

Botswana: 56.3 male, 52.6 female.

Burkina Faso: 53.4 male, 57.6 female.

Her phone rang at Cambodia. She snatched it up in relief, checking the number. Theo. She hesitated. It was always a long talk with Theo. Did she desperately want or desperately *not* want to talk to him? Could she actually pull off an even halfway normal conversation right now? She answered on the sixth ring.

"Oh good," he said, "you're up. Thought you were. I was walking home from Quinn's *lame* party, and I saw your light."

"Nice being a *guy* so you can walk at night," Sophie said. Did her voice sound okay? It didn't to her, but Theo didn't seem to notice. She'd considered wandering the neighborhood, walking the night away. The air, the movement would've felt good, but after that woman got attacked four blocks away a couple of weeks ago, fear kept her in. Inside, a different fear kept her company.

"You didn't miss anything. Totally dead. And *cold*. Look at my hands! Okay, you can't see them because you hate FaceTime (see, I remembered!), but they're *blue*. Bluish. So, can't sleep? Or just reading all that shit you read?"

"Just … reading. And I don't read *shit*." Flicker of guilt at the magazine stash under the bed.

"Only the very highest of highbrow lit'rature for Miss Sophronia." He butchered an English accent. "I know. Okay, back to me. I just did something stupid: texted that girl I told you about, the rude one? I know, I know, you're thinking 'Theo, you dumb *shit*,' but she was at the party and *not* rude and here's the thing …"

Theo launched into his story. It was a familiar one; she couldn't keep up with Theo's crushes. Sophie's eyes dropped to the almanac.

Cambodia: life expectancy 62 male, 67.1 female.

Chad: 49.0 male (*Oh dear God! 49! Under 50*), 51.5 female.

"… then she says all flirty (I *think*), 'maybe give me a call.'

What's that really *mean* though? That 'maybe.' It's that *maybe* …"

Congo (55.8 and 58.9), then a spate of higher life expectancies, then Guinea Bissau (48.6 and 52.7).

How is there such unfairness in the world? How did I not know?

"… which makes me think she might be into me. *Maybe.* Right? *Hey! Ronny!*" Theo raised his voice plaintively on her nickname. She was "Ronny" to Theo, "Sophie" to everyone else. "Sophronia," her much-hated full name, was a grimly guarded secret only Theo knew. "Seriously baring my soul here, and I get nothing. You there?"

"Sorry. Here. Good." She tried to focus. "I mean, it's *good* that she's texting …"

"That's what *I* thought! Because when it's just, like, dead air, even *I* understand that shit, right?"

"Right," Sophie said, forcing a snort of a laugh. *Could I sound more fake?* "Dead air. Bad sign."

"And it's not like I'm high-maintenance. You know me: so low-maintenance I'm, like, barely even *there* …"

Riiight, Theo.

Theo's voice receded as Sophie jumped country to country. Haiti (61.2 and 66.4), Kiribati (63.7 and 68.8), Mozambique (52.6 and 54.1), Zambia (50.8 and 54.1), and finally Zimbabwe (57.3 and 58.7).

She closed the almanac and smoothed a trembling hand over the embossed cover.

"*Ronny!*" She jumped. "You still there? Wait, are you, like, *reading* while I'm talking?" Theo sounded exasperated. "You are, aren't you?"

"No, Theo, I'm not." Which was not, right at this minute, a lie. "I'm … just here. Listening."

"Seriously? Why're you sounding all … robotic or something? Yes. No. Good. Fine. I mean, thanks for listening (if you are) but what's *up* with you?" His voice sharpened. "You okay?"

Sophie felt tears blur her eyes at the question.

People in the world are dying so young, Theo. And Theo, I have something to tell you. Someday. Not now …

"I'm good." Sophie was leaning over, elbows on knees, head in hands. "Just tired. Sorry, not a ton of fun here. I better go."

"You go, get some sleep. Recharge that battery, robo-girl. *Breep-breep.* Joke. I'll let you know if I call 'maybe' girl."

"You better." Sophie tried to inject some emotion, *something* into her voice. "Absolutely. 'Night Theo."

"Later, Ronny."

When he hung up, she wanted him back.

Theo, how have I lived sixteen years of my life thinking I'm owed — what? — ninety of them? (She opened the almanac and flipped to the United States entry for Life Expectancy. 82.2 years for females). *82.2 years, Theo. More than in so many countries. I've assumed 82.2 years at least, a long story of a life, spun out leisurely, one chapter at a time, read slowly, pondered.*

Sophie's heart had started hammering again.

Life-ex-pec-tan-cy, life-ex-pec-tan-cy …

She pressed her fingers hard against her mouth, stifling an inarticulate cry, an *mmm-mmm* of fear. Her breath felt hot and moist against her cold fingers. Through the skin, she felt teeth, bone, her grinning skull. The parts of her that would outlast the others.

My country: Sophie-land. Life Expectancy: radically altered.

She shut her eyes tight, took a deep, shaky breath in and held it. *Hold it, hold it, hold it.*

Chapter One

SHE WALKED PAST THE HOUSE first, not pausing, shooting it a quick sideways glance. All the lights were on. She followed a row of unfamiliar cars lining the street. Four, maybe five, if you counted that Lexus across the street. Dinner party.

She turned slowly at the hedge at the corner and walked back, hesitating at the turn into the winding walkway. The house was at its best at night when the shadows softened the evidence of perpetual renovation — the enormous yellow junk bin that blocked access to the backyard, the tarp-covered lumber, the topsoil. Set back from the sidewalk, its deep lawn buffering it from the street, the house sat behind two enormous elms. In tonight's gloom, with its windows bright with yellow light, it looked almost cheerful, very nearly welcoming. Liar.

Nowhere else to go, though, and I'm cold.

Loud, annoying people from school had invaded the public library to work on a group project, and even with earplugs, she hadn't been able to block them out to read. She watched them covertly and obsessively for almost an hour from her carrel, the two girls scream-laughing at anything the good-looking guy said, the silent foreign exchange student smiling, trying to keep up, the girl with glasses and lank hair somehow getting saddled with doing all the actual work. Sophie finally shoved her novel in her backpack and headed to the mall.

The bench on the second floor outside of London Towne Imports was usually her bench. A quiet place to read or to work on the novel she was furtively writing in a series of black notebooks that she kept at the back of her closet. She was considering calling it *The Black Notebooks*. It was a long-term project that was totally disorganized, a jumble of writing, drawing, arrows, diagrams, plotlines. She was currently focused on making lists of the qualities of her various characters. Damon, she'd decided, was a capital letters DOUCHE.

But the bench was occupied by the old guy with the pushable oxygen tank. She waved to him, and he smiled, gasped, and waved back. Bench after bench was occupied, some familiar people, some not. Everybody seemed to be killing time, sitting somewhere warm. Sophie headed for the food court. Theo had started a new job at Parthenon Greek Eats, and maybe he had a break soon.

He was looking down at his phone as she came up to the counter. She marveled, not for the first time, at his thick, long, dark eyelashes. She would have killed for eyelashes like that.

"Wow, service here *sucks*," she said.

He looked up, flashed his big smile that showed a lot of gums, and pocketed his phone.

"Ronny, thank *God*. I'm dying here. You're my excuse for a break." He lowered his voice conspiratorially. "You're *upset*, got it?"

"Got it. Distraught. Cute hair net, by the way," she whispered.

"Alex!" Theo called to the guy in the back. "Can I take five? It's slow, and I gotta help my friend." He grimaced. "She's dealing with something, you know ..."

"*Please*," Sophie said urgently, blinking hard, "I really need to talk to Theo." The older guy's eyes flicked coldly over her, then dropped to his phone.

"Okay. *Five*. But then you stay after to make it up."

"Nice guy," whispered Sophie as they sat at a table in the food court.

"Total *asshole*. Treats me like dirt. Literal *dirt*. And it's not because I'm Black; I thought that at first, but then he hires Amy — there, that one, the moody-looking, uber-white redhead just coming back from her break — and he treats *her* like shit too, even worse than he treats me."

Sophie glanced back at Alex, who was talking loudly to a sullen-looking Amy as she shrugged back into her Parthenon vest.

"Jeez," said Sophie. "Reaming her out. Why's he so mean?"

"No clue, Ronny. Don't care. But wait! There's more: he seriously expects me to *shout* at people walking by, drum up business. Souvlaki! Gyros! I mean, what the *hell*? If they want Greek, they'll get Greek, right? And if they want, like, Chinese, they're not going to want me screaming at them about Greek food. Plus, I'm a vegetarian, right? Don't make a big deal about it, right? But have you noticed that big-ass, stinking *tower of mystery meat* Parthenon has going on? Basically, a full dead cow, a hot *carcass* revolving right there beside me at the counter. Disgusting. And lamb? You can't even let that little baby sheep grow up before you slaughter it? That is *immoral*, Ronny." He took a breath.

"You done?"

"I could go on, believe me. I gotta get out of this job, Ronny. It's horrible, the worst. Hey, *you* want a job?"

"Tempting, you make it sound so tempting …" She laughed.

"No seriously, you'd rock the hair net." He pulled it off and tried to wrestle it onto her head. There was an undignified scuffle as she fended him off. "But, flip side, I can just see you spilling every single drink." Theo mimed holding a lurching tray. Her clumsiness was legendary among Theo's family.

"Mean," Sophie pointed out, "yet possibly truthful." Recent incidents flickered through her mind: bruising her hip from colliding with the kitchen countertop, that near-fall on the school steps, scrabbling for dropped books on the classroom floor. "So anyway, just quit."

"Got the job five days ago," he said. "Mom would kill me."

Seemed like longer than five days, Sophie thought, that Theo had bitched to her about this job.

"She wouldn't want you to be treated like dirt. And the lamb stuff. There are other jobs." What did she know? She'd never had a job, other than babysitting the little girl next door. She wondered uneasily how broke Theo was. She remembered his bitterness once when he'd said, "We're not all rich like you, Ronny. We can't all just *read* and *write novels* and *eat chocolates* like you can."

"There aren't many, Ronny."

Theo looked around at the depressing food court: a few loners, a couple of lonely seniors, several families with screaming toddlers. Sophie was trying to think of a tactful way to offer him some cash.

"Theo," she said carefully, "I have —"

"Shhh. Ronny, just listen. You hear this song?" he interrupted, pointing with his finger as though the song was hovering right above his head. "You *hear* that shit, Ronny? Heard that one probably seventeen times since I started my shift. Oldies loop."

"*God.* Now *that* is truly horrific. You should have opened with that one."

"Silva!" Alex, the manager at Parthenon Greek Eats, yelled over, pointing at his watch.

"Be right there," Theo called. They got up.

"Lamb souvlaki, fresh and tender!" Alex called out to two passing shoppers.

Theo closed his eyes.

"Yeah, you know what," he said, peeling off his blue and white Parthenon vest, "screw this. Let's go."

He waited until Alex had turned away to the grill and tossed the vest on the counter. It landed by Amy, who barely looked up from her phone. Theo and Sophie ran for the doors.

"Free!" Sophie said as she grabbed Theo's hand, gave it a little squeeze and held on.

"Yes!" he said, breathing deeply. "Don't even feel remotely bad about that one. Made the car wash job look like paradise. The only job I ever liked was that camp counselor one, *loved* that job, but that was only for summer. Those kids were hilarious ..." They skipped the bus and walked home through the dusk, laughing and talking, Theo regaling her with camp stories. Sophie wished for the millionth time that they went to the same school. *But maybe if they did,* she thought, *it would be weird.* Theo was a grade older and had a group of friends she didn't know very well. They were neighborhood friends, house-down-the-street friends, growing-up friends.

Theo's house on the corner of their street was dark.

"Thank God everyone's out," Theo said. "I can be alone. Quiet. Oh, Ronny, if Mom asks about the job, I'm blaming you, okay? She loves *you*. Text you later, buddy." He hugged her and ran up the walk. At the door, he turned.

"Hey. I've been all me, me, me. Sorry. How are you?" he called.

"Upset! Distraught!" she called back, and he laughed and waved.

She looked after him, still warmed by his casual hug, longing for the refuge of that warm, crowded, crumbling, chaotic house she'd been in and out of since she was a little girl. The laughing banter, the packaged cookies, the actual playground *slide* bolted on the stairs that whisked you down to the boy-smelling basement, the frozen pizzas, the bickering, the thrillers and mysteries on the shelves, the chance of seeing even a glimpse of Theo's brother, Calvin.

There was nowhere left to go but home.

SHE WALKED PAST THE HOUSE, counted the cars, walked up to the next corner, steeled herself, and walked back. She stumbled going up the last of the four steps, caught herself, and stood facing the door. It was the original door, from 1921. Carefully restored, like the inner doors, floors, and ceilings.

Tightening her hold on her backpack, she gripped the cold door handle, turning it carefully, slowly, until it unlatched. A small click, more felt than heard. She pushed the door a few inches wide, tilted her head, and listened. A gust of voices, one woman's shrill laugh, the clink of cutlery on dishes, the smell of potpourri mingling with cigarettes and flowers, the tang of unfamiliar perfume and cologne. Voices and shoes indicated ten, twelve people.

At the next burst of laughter, she slipped into the house in one controlled, practiced movement — her right hand grabbing the inner handle as her left released the outer, noiselessly shutting the door behind her. She was in.

She caught a glimpse of herself in the gilt-framed entrance mirror. Tall, big-eyed, thick hair curling over the shoulders of her army surplus jacket. Furtive, comically stealthy, absurdly caught in the act of breaking into her own house. She shook off her Doc Martens and slid down to sit on the step leading down to the long hall, her elbows on her knees, settling in to wait. She had to have some cover before she could risk the dash across the hall to the stairs and up to the sanctuary of her room. That one archway was the bitch. Only about six feet wide, but straight sight lines through to the dining room.

And she couldn't bear her mother or father catching a glimpse of her, hailing her in to be introduced, willing her to say something smooth and literary and witty. She'd had a lifetime of being presented, scrutinized, judged, and dismissed by casual dinner guests. Year after year, and it never got better. Those excruciating adolescent years had been killers — at twelve or thirteen, she'd been all greasy hair, acne, and crippling self-consciousness.

But even now, at sixteen, she seized up thinking of the polite pause, the laser-focus stares, the critical regard of accomplished people, her parents' watchful, warning eyes. Someone inevitably would say she must be a straight-A English student, *haha*! With her family history, she should be *teaching* that class, *haha*! Always, always the same. Standing there squirming while her mother or father described their ideal version of her ("Sophronia is an accomplished writer in her own right"), conscious of her height, her baggy clothes, her lack of accomplishment. Desperate, *desperate* to be released.

I will not do it anymore. I won't. I refuse.

She picked out snatches of conversation. Different people than two nights ago. She studied the buckle of a fashionable pair of women's boots.

"… Nickleby! Elisabeth, you lit-geek! Do you have another cat named Copperfield?"

"… really a phenomenal specimen of the craft. Phe*nom*enal …"

"… which are, of course, original. Milanese." That last was her father's voice, with its slight hint of an English accent retained from an eight-month master's degree in Oxford almost thirty years ago.

He was boring people about the house again, Sophie knew. She'd heard many, many, too many times about the Milanese light sconces in the dining room. Their guests probably had as well. Her father was eternally, painstakingly restoring the house, at least the areas company would see. This absorbing hobby — fighting with contractors, leafing through samples, comparing tile and wallpaper, writing massive checks — occupied most of her father's time when he wasn't lawyering or running.

Meanwhile, behind the original, exquisite oak swing door to the dining room, Sophie ate breakfast standing up in a cramped kitchen with a broken, moldy, tiled floor and sagging counters. Warped windows let in a year-round breeze in the tiny bedrooms upstairs, and a steep, neck-breaking, rickety flight of bare wooden servants' stairs led down to the washer/dryer, the freezer, and the carefully selected cache of imported wine. Further into the basement cave, a ragged-edged remnant of carpet covered bare concrete, and two ancient sofas sagged around a television. Nothing as tacky as a TV would ever have sat in the elegant, spacious Gayle-St. John drawing room among the mahogany bookshelves.

"What's the vintage, did you say?" Nameless, polite guest.

Suck up, thought Sophie.

Murmur, murmur, murmur. Clink, clink. Sophie picked at a small flaw in the hall's Turkish carpet, and coaxed and pulled until a long, maroon strand unraveled, scraping a naked path until it broke. Sophie carefully slipped it into her pocket and scuffed her foot along the empty line in the carpet. She wondered where Nick was, then figured he'd probably been shut in her room just before the company arrived.

She transferred her attention to her hands. She picked and gnawed at a hangnail on her right thumb, biding her time for the cover of noise that would free her.

Wait.

She paused, lifted her head, stopped nibbling a piece of skin with her front teeth. That voice. That dry, precise, low rumble.

Oh, God, is that Mariam? Why is she here? Nobody told me she was coming.

Sophie bit more savagely at the hangnail, tasting blood, straining her ears. Yes. It was her grandmother, she was sure of it, not so much from the voice but from the complete, electric silence from everyone else. When the Great Lady spoke, nobody interrupted.

Sophie could just see her: hunched in her chair, picking at her food with long fingers, brooding, preoccupied, deliberately rude, the sweep of her trademark long, straight, black hair (*Still jet black. Give it up, old lady*) framing the famous angular face, the hawkish profile. Then the deliberate domination of the conversation, her cold, contemptuous eyes raised in boredom or battle, her low voice spinning out a story to a room of people listening in rapt, reverential silence. The audience, intensely conscious of her genius and notoriety, of being favored, of being at An Event, hungrily devoured the details, already mentally framing their own recounting of it.

"Well, she's brilliant of course. Inaccessibly brilliant. Profound ..."

"Penetrating. *Razor* sharp. Stripped us all bare in the space of three seconds ..."

"Terrifying, positively terrifying. Five times married and how many ... dalliances? Brave, doomed men. Seventy if she's a day, but she has something still ..."

Sophie had heard it all before. She knew, for example, that at tonight's dinner, as at all Mariam-dinners, there would be one or two foolhardy souls, their hands locked around their wine glasses, who were rehearsing smooth, witty, literary rejoinders behind attentive faces. *They never learned*, Sophie thought wearily. *They never grasped the essential fact that this was not a conversation.* No normal give-and-take, no exchange of ideas, no back-and-forth. They were body-props for Mariam's performance, if she chose to perform. None of them mattered to Mariam. Nobody ever had.

Sophie waited, her forehead on her knees, rocking slightly. She wondered which Mariam would they get tonight. Once, with Theo, she'd ticked off on her fingers how many Mariams there were (that she knew of).

"The grande dame literary icon, the cause-of-the-day pseudo-activist, the foul-mouthed anti-establishment writer ..."

"Okay, so far that one's my favorite!" Theo had said, clearly delighted.

"... the man-hater, the Marxist, the contrarian —"

"Stop, please stop. So *many* of your bitchy old granny ..."

Which had Mariam decided on tonight, Sophie wondered, as she sat, coiled in her chair, abstracted and detached? Depended on her mood, or maybe on the audience. Was this party people from the law firm? From the English department? Government Department of Arts and Culture? People to cultivate, people to shock, people to use, people to snub?

Alison Hughes

Murmur, murmur. The gravelly, smoker's voice continued low and uninterrupted. A story, Sophie decided. Ah,
storyteller-Mariam.

Sophie raised then dropped her head on her knees. The bang
of forehead on kneecap felt good. She banged it again.

"… positively moronic … of any *adult*" (ripple of laughter)
"… putrid, unutterably putrid … as if their little country *mattered*
to one …"

Another voice, male, asking a deferential question. Cut off
rudely by Mariam, her voice inching louder.

"And I told the president that, considering it *very* seriously, I
didn't give a *flying fuck*," Mariam enunciated clearly.

Punch line, aaand cue: hysterical laughter, thought Sophie,
jumping to her feet, securing her hold on her bag, and coiling for
the sprint.

Hysterical laughter.

Head down, arm out for the banister that helped to pull her
stumbling feet up faster, she bolted for the stairs.

Chapter Two

AN HOUR LATER, THERE WAS a knock on her bedroom door. Sprawled on her bed in sweats, Sophie shoved her novel and notepad under her pillow, stuffed an empty bag of chips under her bed, flipped open her Legal Studies text, and grabbed her cell phone. She held it to her ear and turned to the door, her heart pounding. It wouldn't be Mariam. Mariam had never come up to her room. Never. Not once. And even if for some reason she ever *did*, Sophie guessed she wouldn't knock. She was a burster-inner, for sure. Maybe even a kicker-inner.

Another knock, a little louder. Sophie relaxed. It was her mom, of course. The tentative double-knocker.

"What?" Sophie said.

Her mother opened the door, holding out a plate covered in foil.

"Brought you some food. Oh, you're —" She gestured to the phone. She was wearing what Sophie thought of as her "artsy-boho outfit," a long, expensive, unflattering, sludge-green dress that showed a lot of bony chest, embroidered blouse, three strings of beads, dangly earrings swinging against her scrawny neck. Literary crowd. The law firm people would never have gotten the beads.

Her mother slipped into the room, shutting the door quickly against Nickleby, who tried to bolt. He had an unerring radar for the one person in the room who hated cats, and with feline perverseness, would lock in on them, winding around their legs, settling in their lap.

"Yeah, okay. Look, just a sec," she said to the dead phone, then smothered it on her shoulder. Sophie raised her eyebrows pointedly. "Thanks, Mom, just put it anywhere. Who'd you get for the food?"

"Dolce Vita," her mother murmured, frowning as she looked for a spot for the plate in all the mess. She finally propped it on a pile of books on the nightstand and turned, pushing up her new glasses. Sophie's heart had sunk at those glasses; Prada, but oh, so horrible on her, the stark, heavy, round frames making her head with the maroon pixie cut look even bigger, more bobble-headed on her tiny shoulders. Sophie had spanned her mother's thin wrist with a thumb and forefinger when she was ten years old. She'd towered over her at twelve.

"Mariam's here," her mother said, fingering her beads tensely. Even her daughter called her *Mariam,* a fact which annoyed Sophie irrationally. Never *Mom* or *Mother* or even *Ma.* Sophie would have loved her mother to call Mariam *Ma.*

Their eyes met.

"You okay?" Sophie asked.

"It's just for dinner. She's not staying."

She never stayed with them in their house like other grandparents presumably did. "Mariam needs her space," her mother would say. She always blew in, holed up in some hotel, and left sometimes without a word. But did "not staying" mean she was only in town for a few days? Or weeks? *Please, not weeks. There's always less air when Mariam is in town.*

"Thank *God*."

"Don't. She showed up rather unexpectedly with a new friend when we were having drinks before dinner," she said. "Not terribly convenient because I ordered dinner for ten, but Gordon and Sylvia, you know the early moderns? They're over the *moon*."

"Yeah, because they don't *know* Granny Dearest," said Sophie. "I think I'm going to start calling her 'Granny.' She'd love that! How about you start calling her 'Ma'? You know, 'Ma, stop with the stories,' or 'could you help me with the dishes, Ma?' In front of everybody! Now *that* would be funny. I think that would be hi*lar*ious."

Her mother looked down, a little smile playing around her lips.

"Oh, she'd absolutely hate that," her mother murmured.

"Which is exactly the point! Anyway, thanks for the warning."

Sophie watched her mother clear a layer of dust off an old snow globe with one bony finger, one line at a time. She picked up the globe and idly shook it.

"Look, Mom, I'm actually on the *phone* here, remember? Fiona."

"Oh. Right. Sorry."

Sophie pretended to talk until she heard the creak of her mother's footsteps receding down the hall. The footsteps hesitated at the top of the stairs and then went on quickly to the bedroom at the end of the hall.

Going to hide from Mariam in her room for a little longer, Sophie thought. A wave of sympathy for her mother washed over her. Bad enough being Mariam's granddaughter; she couldn't even imagine how it had been being her daughter. The constant criticism, the absences, the life lived in another person's shadow.

She herself was not hiding from Mariam. She was deliberately, uncaringly *avoiding*. She was just living. She pulled her novel from under the covers. *Our Mutual Friend*. Charles Dickens's last work, apparently. She was appalled at the character she'd been named after: Sophronia, a wheedling, flattering, scheming fortune-hunter. But she was probably just obscure enough to give her mother some kind of pathetic street cred at the English department.

Dickens was her mother's specialty, her PhD thesis, her publication gold mine, her upper-year seminars, her property, her baby. Sophie knew that within twenty seconds of her mother knowing she was reading Dickens, she would have hauled our mutual friend off by his high collar, and gutted, dissected, and ruined him for her.

"From what you say, it seems like Dickens is her whole identity," Sophie's friend Fiona had once said in her dry, precise voice.

"I know. It's weird," Sophie had said.

"No, not really. It's *sad*."

Sophie always remembered that. It sometimes made her more patient with her mother when she drove Sophie crazy. Like when they adopted Nickleby. Sophie had begged for years for a pet, and was finally allowed a declawed, hypoallergenic, non-shedding one. But her mother said that if "the creature" was to be in the house, potentially among guests, he was going to have a conversation-starter name. Oliver Twist. Little Dorrit. Nicholas Nickleby. Sophie had wanted the cat, *needed* the cat, and so was forced to compromise. She called the cat *Nick*.

Dickens was also to blame for her middle name, Havisham. Miss Havisham was another of his characters — a sad, weird old lady who was jilted at the altar and wore her decaying wedding dress everywhere. Perfect namesake for an innocent young girl.

Thanks, Mom, for saddling me with Sophronia Havisham Gayle-St. John, which makes me totally squirm whenever I have to write it on anything official.

"Wow. That's seriously your *name*? Uh, very distinctive, very upper crust," Theo had said kindly, that time when she swore him to secrecy.

The "Gayle" part had to be there, of course. Sophie's mother's maiden name, famous Mariam's last name. Mariam hadn't taken any of the names of any of her five husbands, always remaining Mariam Gayle. But Sophie's father had taken the name, he'd fallen over himself to become a hyphenated Gayle-St. John when he married Sophie's mother, shamelessly clutching at the golden threads of Mariam Gayle's fame.

Sophie peeled back the foil from the dinner plate her mother had brought. Sodden, steamed vegetables, one miniscule piece of sole in a teaspoonful of white sauce. Was it that dinner had had to stretch to accommodate two more people, or was this one of her mother's tiny, pointed aggressions? Diet portions? Only she didn't need to diet, Sophie thought angrily, holding the plate close to her mouth, shoveling it in. She was *normal*-sized. Tall, sure, tallish. But otherwise just normal.

Her mother had inherited Mariam's elfin build, but whereas Mariam walked like a dancer and had a face whose strong, arched lines settled in arrogant disdain, a face that had appeared on the cover of every major magazine in the world, Sophie's mother, Elisabeth, blinked and scuttled, peered, poked, and fidgeted.

Sophie was glad she had inherited nothing of Mariam, other than maybe her eye color, which was a clear slate gray (Gayle eyes). Sophie took after her father's side of the family: tall, big hands and feet, straight dark brows and heavy, curling brown hair. She had the vivid coloring of the St. Johns, naturally red lips, embarrassment or exertion staining hectic vertical lines in her cheeks. But it was inferior, all of it. The ideal of feminine beauty in the Gayle family was and always would be Mariam's: anemic, tiny, bony. Mariam made the rules. Mariam set the standard.

Sophie had learned this very early. She'd been six or seven years old, tallest in her ballet class, practicing her routine in the kitchen. Slide, slide, first position, slide, graceful twirl … Mariam, taking a short break between husbands, had sat at the table, eyeing her critically through a haze of cigarette smoke. Long drag, short, impatient exhale.

"Sophronia lumbers like a St. John. There's nothing Gayle about her," Mariam had said, stubbing out the cigarette, mouth twisted in disgust. Sophie's mother, washing fruit at the sink, had looked at Sophie, not in apology or allegiance, but in assessment. There was something else there, too. Wariness. Worry. Fear? Why had her mother looked afraid?

"Hardly *lumbers*, Mariam. She doesn't *lumber*."

"Have you ever *watched* the child? Watch her." Mariam gestured with a lit cigarette. "Get her to do another of those tippy-toe twirls. Botches those like you wouldn't believe."

But ballet was already over for Sophie. She'd run out of the room, smacking her shoulder painfully against the door jamb. All through soccer leagues or swimming lessons, through painful school gym times, during games at recess, any time she felt awkward or clumsy, instances happening with increasing regularity, she thought of that throwaway, unthinking, cruel, formative remark: "Sophronia lumbers like a St. John."

At age nine, Sophie dropped the "–ronia" and "Gayle" altogether and became, belligerently, Sophie St. John, a proud, defiant lumberer.

Chapter Three

CRYSTAL, THE SIX-YEAR-OLD WHO LIVED two doors down, was on her haunches by the bus stop the next morning, peering at the gutter drain crusted over with spring debris.

"Muck," she said as Sophie walked up, poking a stick in and hoisting a wad of dead grass and mud, holding it out as proof.

"Yeah. You got that right."

Sophie looked down at the bent head on her thin neck, static-fine dark hair sticking to the little face, a trail of grime on her cheek where it had been swept back by a grubby hand. She'd been Crystal's babysitter since Crystal was a baby, mesmerized by Crystal's fuzzy, sweet-smelling head and the delicate, blue-tinged hollows by her temples that were too soft and vulnerable to be safe. She had memories of that first New Year's Eve, holding Crystal for six hours straight, her arms aching, easing down into a chair to take the pressure off her back, the baby a dead, sweaty, spent weight. But she couldn't bring herself to entrust the baby to the sharp perils of her wicker bassinet.

"I like your boots," Sophie said, giving Crystal's muddy boot a nudge with her foot.

Crystal looked down.

"Pink. They used to have Little Kitty on them, but she's mostly scraped off now. That's where one of her eyes was." She used the muddy stick to stab at the faded dot.

Sophie picked up a stick and poked at the drain, delaying her walk to school so that she could get there right when the bell rang.

"Why don't *you* ever wear pink? Why only black? Black everything," Crystal spoke as she piled up a dam of muck. "Black, black, black."

Sophie glanced down at her boots, black jeans, black T-shirt, black hoodie.

"Sometimes I wear some white," Sophie said. "A T-shirt or something. Oh, and army green. I don't know, Crystal. Sometimes black just feels right."

"I don't like your *hair* black."

"Nah, wasn't my best look." The dyed-black brush cut had been a serious mistake. Thank God her hair grew quickly.

They both saw the worm at the same time, long and thin and pale, shooting down the gutter stream toward the drain.

"Shit! Watch it!" Sophie dropped her backpack and took a quick, crouching step in.

Crystal coolly dumped a load of muck onto the dam in the worm's path.

The worm hinged awkwardly on the debris. Sophie cupped a handful of cold worm-filth and threw it onto the brown lawn across the sidewalk, rubbing her hand on the grass to clean it. She peered anxiously at the lump on the grass, worried that the rescue might have backfired, impaling or crushing the soft, bloated body. But as she watched, the worm began to ooze into the lawn.

"Hey, look, Crystal! Look! I think he'll make it. Don't worry," Sophie said.

Crystal looked over at her, her face expressionless.

"That happens a lot. There's lots of worms. Some are alive but some aren't. And some are only *half* a worm, sometimes."

"Well, you try to save them, right, Crystal? You help them out, right? Even the half-worms. Maybe even *especially* the half-worms." Sophie eyed her anxiously.

Crystal shrugged.

"Sometimes. But there's lots of them. Some just go down the drain. They don't seem to mind."

SOPHIE SLIPPED IN THE SIDE door just as the bell rang, put her head down, and ran-walked straight to Room 107, first door on the left. Since that stupid altercation with Emily Henday, she'd been forbidden the use of her locker. One more part of the school that was closed off to her, one less fight to have. It was all so petty, but Emily had started it.

"She holds it wiiide open, like this." Sophie swung an imaginary locker to show Fiona. "Like, my locker is right next to hers. Isn't there some kind of locker etiquette shit that says you stay in your locker-lane? I have to wait until she's completely done and gone to get to my locker."

"Just say something, then," Fiona said. "It's going to drive you crazy if you don't."

It was good advice that Sophie ignored. Tired of waiting, convinced she was being baited, simmering with anger, Sophie finally reached into her locker and pushed the door back hard. Emily's locker door had slammed shut on her hand. The principal hadn't listened to her side, or to her concession that it might have been joint stupidity. Of course, the one with the bloody hand got all the sympathy. And the other had to clear out her locker.

Adnan was having a bad morning, yipping and flapping

over in his corner. Lucy was crouched in front of him, running through the strategies. She put her face near his, gestured, and grabbed his hand, her other hand snaking behind her to hitch up jeans that had ridden down to reveal the butterfly tattoo on the small of her ample back.

Wayne gave Sophie a stinging high five as she passed and then resumed rattling off stats from the hockey game to Grace, who stared straight ahead, her vacant gaze unresponsive.

"There's an assembly." Fiona sidled up to Sophie, wringing her hands with sanitizer. "This morning. Right after the bell. Why don't they *tell* us they're going to do this so we can prepare?" Fiona slid into her seat, swiveled to check that her backpack was hooked on her chair, then checked again. She swallowed, looking at Sophie with wide, intense eyes.

"Shit. Ah well, we'll live through it." Sophie's reassuring tone was automatic as she dumped her heavy backpack and peeled off her hoodie.

"With the whole school. Everyone."

"I hate those."

"Me *too*," Fiona said earnestly, straining toward Sophie. "The smell. The *germs*. Just imagine the germs on the floor, let alone in the *air*. Everyone there breathing. In one room. In and out, in and out. *God*. And the crush of people ..."

Fiona was almost completely colorless: a pale, pinched face, bleached pale blue eyes, a high forehead merging into pale, limp, straight blond hair. *She has a skeleton-face when she's stressed*, Sophie thought in alarm.

"Fed Morton yet?" Sophie asked. She'd learned that a dexterous change of subject sometimes snapped Fiona out of her tailspin of anxiety.

Fiona blinked.

"I forgot. How could I *forget*?"

"It's not like he's watching the clock, Fi. C'mon."

Morton, the class betta fish, was circling peevishly in his bowl, a fluid, fierce ribbon stripe of bluish-purple and red. Morton, the glamour boy, the tough guy who puffed out ferociously when confronting himself in a mirror, couldn't seem to eat naturally in a fish-like way on his own. They'd watched for a good three days, helpless, as he thrashed and flailed, choked and regurgitated as if the dead, dried worm-bits he was trying to swallow were fighting back. Then Sophie and Fiona had figured out a palliative-care strategy. It was Sophie who had tried first to feed him by hand, corralling him in the hacked off bottom half of a water bottle, her shaky hands alarming the fish, slopping water and spilling worm meal all over the counter. Once Lucy had brought in a package of plastic gloves, Fiona took over.

Sophie leaned on the counter as Fiona spread out a paper towel and arranged in precise, surgical order plastic gloves, fish food, glass, strainer, and tweezers. She snapped on the gloves, scooped up some aquarium water in the glass, then neatly caught the darting streak of blue and red. Tweezing a bit of worm meal, she dangled it near Morton, who stilled. When he was close enough and opened his ugly mouth, she neatly stuffed the piece deep. Piece by painstaking piece, Morton was saved. Sophie watched Fiona's delicate hands, all three of them calmed by the daily ritual.

He's a screwup, too, thought Sophie, watching the graceful plume slide to the surface, the bulldog mouth choke down another dried worm-bit.

"Guy's a fighter," murmured Fiona. "Aren't you, Mort?"

AT THE ASSEMBLY THEY ENDURED every verse of the school song, breathily belted out by Tamara Stepchuk and Ashleigh Kaminski, girls with perfect hair who knew it.

One special time … to be and to grow … one special place … to learn and to know …

Wide eyes, practiced manipulation of the microphone, sliding it away during the belt-it-out portions, nestling it in close for the breathy bits. Harmony, too. The girls were giving it their best.

Who *writes* this crap? Sophie wondered, sitting cross-legged and hunched over, scribbling with a pen on her jeans. Peace and love and friendship and togetherness, that kind of shit. She wondered if anyone could have ever thought that that was an accurate representation of how high school operates. She couldn't believe anyone who'd ever set foot in any high school could believe that. It must be aspirational, she decided, feel-good, like the national anthem of a failing, crime-ridden country.

Helping each other … our hearts and our minds … caring and sharing … let our light shiiiine …

Big finish on the imperfect rhyme, girls, Sophie thought, looking furtively around the gym through the heavy bank of her hair, her face blank. Her glance slid over other raised faces, some polite, some assessing, some embarrassed. The girls with the hard eyes and perfect clothes. The loud girls, the dramatic ones, the Ashleigh and Tamara girls. The boys who liked girls like that, the sports guys who looked right past you as though you were nothing, not a person, not female, not anything. The less attractive, nicer guys who looked away. One girl a few rows back caught Sophie's eye and smiled. Sophie ignored her deliberately, sliding her glance away as though their eyes had never met, as though she'd always been looking over the girl's shoulder.

I will cheat you, nice girl, out of your cheap and easy sympathy. I will show you your kindness is not kindness, it is a craving for power and virtue, from appearing to support the school freaks. I will force you to admit that we can be assholes too.

After this small spurt of defiance, Sophie felt a wave of supreme indifference. She had no real connection with anyone outside her class at this school; she felt remote from them all, islanded, isolated, Room 107'd. She glanced quickly down the line at her classmates from the Opportunity Class, the Op-Shop. They were the only reasons she stayed, her weird friends, her home base as she took some regular classes.

Adnan was swaying and clapping to the music, his agitation forgotten. His eyes were closed, his thin dark face was rapt. Wayne smiled gently, looking down at his thick body, shaking his head and crossing and uncrossing his short arms, an inscrutable look on his wide face. Grace sat stock-still, her head sunk back on her neck like a pelican in flight, dead shark-eyes facing forward but seeing God only knows what, hands loose in her lap, her body, at least, here and accounted for.

Fiona huddled against Sophie, her hands held in the air like a freshly gloved surgeon, trying not to touch anything. Sophie could feel the crackling waves of her tension, could almost smell her anxiety.

"Fi, put your hands down," Sophie whispered, and shifted position on the dusty gym floor, putting a few inches between them.

"Oh, sorry." Fiona turned and lowered her hands slightly, tucking in her elbows. Sophie glanced over, exasperated. She wasn't sure if she hadn't preferred the neurotic surgeon to the alert prairie dog look Fiona had now. She glanced back over her shoulder. That bitch was still trying to catch her eye, still smiling supportively. Demanding connection, gratitude, submission, *something*. Sophie ignored her.

The principal, Mr. Nguyen, rushed over to congratulate the singers.

"Stellar job, Ashleigh and Tamara! Just great! A wonderful lead-in to 'April is Arts,' where our school will celebrate the dramatic, literary, and performing arts. Ms. Sharma has put together a really awesome PowerPoint of our past performances —" he fiddled awkwardly with the computer "— our thespian triumphs —" the computer stubbornly refused to give up the PowerPoint. He finally found it, the lights dimmed, and a scene from last year's production of *Annie* sprang up on the wall.

"Everyone, up, up, up," Ms. Linden gestured to the Op-Shop class, making scooping motions with her arms. "Back to class," she hissed in the kind of whisper that is louder than a low voice, turning to lead the way, bending awkwardly, obsequiously, to avoid the projector light. This was their cue to melt inconspicuously from the gym. Ms. Linden's policy for assemblies was "come late and leave early." It was supposed to alleviate anxiety and stress about entering and leaving with the rest of the school, about mingling in a crush with all the normal kids. It was supposed to be about them. Inclusion in action.

Adnan, stumbling to his feet, eyes riveted on the *Annie* slides, said loudly, "Tomorrow. The sun will come out tomorrow." He repeated this earnestly and unmusically as Ms. Linden grabbed his hand and marched him off. Wayne got a big laugh by stopping right in the light and flexing his muscles. Sophie bolted quickly and stumbled a little over a cord, and Fiona and Grace were two slim silhouettes — one tense, one lax, one leading, one willing to go wherever — slipping into and out of the light, one pulling the other by the hand, then wiping it on her jeans.

Chapter Four

TWO MEN IN SUITS BY the door to Room 107 pretended not to watch them wander back from the assembly. This, thought Sophie, explained Ms. Linden's skirt and nylons rather than her usual jeans or yoga pants. Another tour of the Opportunity Class, their "supportive and therapeutic environment for special-needs kids." Another safari.

They were all the same, these funders, these school trustees, these government underlings who drew the short straw; they masked their nervousness or avidity with a hearty and open friendliness, listening with exaggerated intensity and respectful head-tilting to Ms. Linden's tour guide patter, moving around the class, smiling encouragingly if they caught a student's eye, politely admiring the latest art therapy projects. Sophie's was an empty tissue box stuck on its side on a piece of cardboard. She had "arted" it (Wayne's word) yesterday, a bad day, a lowering, headachy day, and scuffling among the raw materials in the bin with the others she had been overcome, paralyzed by the futility of it all.

An immense weariness had washed over her, and she'd grabbed the tissue box and cardboard, the first things to hand, and stumbled back to her desk, putting her head down on her arms, fighting the dark waves.

This desk is here. It's real. The wood is hard. The people you hear talking — there's Lucy laughing, and Adnan repeating and Wayne's quick, garbled speech — they're real. They're here. And, she thought, digging her fingernails into her forearm, *you're real, too, Sophie. Feel that?* She pinched the skin, hard. *Do you feel that?*

Lucy had patted her shoulder, mercifully shooed away the art therapist, and left Sophie alone. It passed. Whatever it was seemed to pass, leaving Sophie feeling like she'd been washed up on a shore after a storm — fragile, tentative, wobbly, weak, and dull. Sophie heard someone come over and she opened her eyes to see Ms. Linden wordlessly deposit a protein bar on her desk. Sophie sat up, fumbled with it, tore it open with her teeth, and wolfed it down, chewing and looking around the room with damp, belligerent, bewildered eyes. A gulp of water from her water bottle and she felt more human.

"You okay?" Fiona had sidled over, her eyes anxious. "You black out again?"

Sophie stirred. Her arms and legs felt stiff.

"Nah. I'm okay, Fi. Thanks." Sophie had looked over at the pile of carefully cut paper on Fiona's desk, remembered it was art therapy, reached for the tissue box and cardboard and stared at them a long time. Her mind felt sluggish. *Focus*, she told herself. *Think. Get a grip.*

Finally, she'd glued the empty box perpendicular, and written *No More Tears* on the cardboard, hoping the minimalist pseu-do-profundity might mask the lack of effort. The art therapist loved it, the trustees were enthralled.

"That's her," she heard one whisper to another. "*Mariam Gayle's* granddaughter!"

An odd girl, she could imagine them saying, *but most likely a genius.*

Just like her grandmother.

THE SCHOOL PRODUCTION OF *CHARLIE and the Chocolate Factory* was in full rehearsal, irritating Oompa Loompas pelting down the halls after school. The Opportunity Class, along with the rest of the school, would be forced to watch the dress rehearsal. It would be talked up as a privilege, presented as a really special treat. Sophie was already planning on being sick that day.

"And this year, for the first time, our Room 107 family will *also* be performing a play," announced Ms. Linden, her strained face splitting into her grimace-grin. She was a tall, thin woman with shoulder-length gray hair, heavy bangs, and a nervous habit of pushing up her thick glasses with her middle finger. She did it now. Sophie wondered if the gesture was subconscious, this repeated giving of the finger to the whole class.

"Not in front of the whole school, though, right? We're not actually performing a play in front of the whole school?" Fiona asked in an immediate panic.

"Oh, no, no," Ms. Linden assured her. "Just any relatives or friends you might choose to bring. Small. Very small. *In*timate." Ms. Linden clutched her hands together tightly, demonstrating how very tiny it would be. "We're rather limited in choice of plays by our small number," she continued, "but I really think I've found a winner for us! It's a very famous play that speaks profoundly about difference, tolerance, and inclusion."

Sophie was scribbling on her binder. There was a moment of silence, and she glanced up. Lucy, the classroom aide, caught her eye, flashed her a warning. Ms. Linden was looking right at her. She couldn't mean …

"And the play has an added significance for this class, particularly for our friend Sophie, whose grandmother wrote the Pulitzer prize-winning novel on which the play is based! It's Mariam Gayle's *Abomination!*"

It never ends, Sophie thought. *Never.*

During her disastrous foray into the school's advanced English class this fall, they'd studied *Abomination*, Mr. Green glancing hopefully, expectantly, at Sophie's stony, hostile face. The year before it had been Mariam's short stories. She'd been approached by teachers and principals, librarians, students, and parents to have her grandmother do a signing, a reading, a workshop, a graduation address, a keynote speech. She'd never passed on the requests, but regretfully refused for her, citing her grandmother's absence, her writing schedule, her world travel, her unspecified "new projects," her famed reclusiveness.

She had, several times, come dangerously close to telling the truth: "Sorry, but I believe she's busy screwing somebody's husband," or "She's in rehab (but that's kind of hush-hush)," or "To be honest, the old hag doesn't give a rat's ass about anybody else, so …"

Abomination, the 2004 novel where Mariam had cemented her literary reputation as the doyenne of "Fantasticanlit," had won a host of national and international awards, and drawn comparisons with Shelley, Kafka, and Márquez.

Sophie hated the story. Abomination is a human baby, born with neither face nor fingers, kept hidden, shrouded always in black, and prone to muffled, existential moaning. Abomination's father, an ill-educated, surly, and menacing figure, refuses to name Abomination or call her anything but "it" or "the monster," a practice both hurtful and awkward in direct address. The townsfolk also revile "the thing-being," page after page, but aside from the odd spate of lobbing deformed vegetables, Abomination grows up relatively unmolested. She discovers an affinity with nature during long chapters where flowers lift their heads as she passes, and rabbits still. But when religious figures plot eradication of "the stain in their midst," Abomination's mother spirits her away to a God-like figure in a celestial courtroom, who, over six chapters, establishes Abomination's humanity. It is at this point that Abomination takes flight, "her faceless face raised to the limitless skies."

At the celebration of her human beingness, Abomination (inexplicably still lacking a better name, but more spiffily dressed in specially designed, colorful veiling) confronts her father in a dignified yet tedious pantomime. He is overcome with shame. She is forgiving. The town is humbled by her decency and humanity. Abomination then slips away with a shadowy, trusted friend who is waiting for her, which may or may not be Death.

The novel ends, of course, with the famous and ambiguous line: "She stumbled, like many before her, groping, faceless face unseeingly seeking the way, her way, away, away into the gathering night." Which never explained why she didn't just fly.

That was the play the Opportunity Class was going to perform.

Christ, thought Sophie, *a real cheerer-upper*. Plus, logistically, old Abby *flies*. Literally *flies*. It's not a metaphor, Mariam's been clear on that at least. *How the hell are we supposed to do that?* She scribbled harder on her binder.

Ms. Linden glanced quickly at Lucy, then at Sophie.

"What do you think of the idea, Sophie? Of doing *Abomination*?"

"Great," Sophie said dully, face closed, not looking up.

You want me to gush and exclaim and thank you for trying to connect. Wow, you have a lot to learn, Ms. Linden.

"Because if it's weird for you, we can switch," said Lucy. "Maybe it's a bit heavy," she said, turning to Ms. Linden.

"Pro*found*," protested Ms. Linden. "Up*lift*ing! Still, we can find something else, of course. Totally up to Sophie."

"It's okay. Whatever."

"Only if you're completely sure ..." Ms. Linden said.

"It's *fine*," Sophie said loudly. Adnan stirred and started flapping at the outburst.

"Okay, okay, good. That's good that it's fine." Ms. Linden smiled her skull-grimace, her hair bobbing as she nodded. "Now, we want this to be *fun*, right? Uplifting. Emphasis on inclusion and community! A way for Room 107 to really come together." She linked her bony fingers together tightly, like she was praying.

She really does try, Sophie thought wearily. *She's a good person. She probably spent weeks thinking about this, and hopes we'll remember it for the rest of our lives.*

"So: casting," Ms. Linden said. "The main characters are Father, Mother, God-Creature, Shadowy Friend, and, of course, Abomination."

"God! I wanna be God!" roared Wayne, elaborately pointing at his chest with both hands and grinning at the others.

"I vote Wayne as God, too," Lucy said, laughing.

"I guess I could be Mother," Fiona volunteered tentatively. "There aren't that many lines, are there? Or do you want Mother, Sophie? Grace?

"Nah, go for it," muttered Sophie. Grace turned her head in that extremely careful way she had, like it would fall off if she moved too quickly, and stared.

"Adnan, how do you feel about being Father?" asked Lucy, tapping his hand, getting him to look at her. "That okay with you? Father?" Adnan barely looked up from the puzzle he was doing. "I think we'll say Adnan is Father," said Lucy.

"So," Ms. Linden said, eyeing Sophie and Grace, "we just need Abomination and Shadowy Friend."

An uncertain silence settled in the room.

"Abomination," said Sophie quickly, "I'll be Abomination." Grace didn't need to be cast in Mariam's shittiest role of all time; none of them did. She turned to Grace. "You okay with Shadowy Friend?" Grace was staring at the wall over Sophie's shoulder.

"Grace!" Sophie said loudly, tapping her shoulder. "You okay with being *Shadowy Friend?* In the play?" Nothing. Blank. Sophie wanted to grab both her shoulders and shake hard. *Anybody home, Grace?*

"I think Grace will do great as Shadowy Friend," said Lucy, her hands on her hips.

"She'll be *awesome!* Wow, I'm super-impressed, Room 107!" Ms. Linden said, with the excessive enthusiasm Sophie found demeaning. Like they were all in kindergarten. "Casting all done in, like, five minutes!"

"There *are* only five of us," Fiona pointed out. "Since Charlie's gone."

Awkward silence. Nobody wanted to think about Charlie and his rages.

Ms. Linden was not to be cheated out of her small triumph.

"*Very* impressed!" she said. "Now, we'll set a date so you can invite your parents and friends. And other relatives if you want." She avoided looking at Sophie. "Aunts, uncles, grandparents …"

Ahh, she wants Mariam to come. She wants it badly. She wants to gush about how big a fan she's been, wants to be the hero of her book club, wants to say she's met the legendary Mariam Gayle. Oh, Ms. Linden, if only you knew ...

Sophie looked down at her binder. Her parents definitely wouldn't be getting an invite to see Room 107 perform Mariam's stupid, overrated story. She could just see them, fastidious, critical, overdressed. Slumming politely with the other parents. Tight, superior little smiles. She would eat the invitation before that happened.

And nothing, not one thing in the whole world, could make her invite Mariam. Ms. Linden would work herself to the bone for this play, but no matter how much they rehearsed, no matter how well it was performed, Mariam would hate it anyway. Nobody deserved Mariam's withering scorn, least of all Ms. Linden, someone actually trying to do some good in this world. It would be like introducing a shark into a crowded swimming pool. It was a relief to know that she'd be long gone by the time they performed the play. Her family had a few days, maybe a week of stress and tension before Mariam, dead-eyed and restless, swam off on the hunt for fresh prey.

Chapter Five

"I THINK WE'RE GOING TO have problems with Linden," Sophie said as she and Fiona walked home. "I've got that feeling."

"She's better than Thorpe," Fiona said, scrupulously avoiding the sidewalk cracks. Not just the regular ones between sections, but the irregular ones, the randoms, the ones made by weather or wear, widened by pushy weeds. They all counted.

"*Obviously*. Boy, *she* left in a hurry, hey? But what do you think of her? Ms. Linden. Why aren't we calling her 'Barbara,' by the way? Power shit? I'm only going to respond to Ms. St. John. *And* I'm calling her Barbara. No, Barb. No, *Babs*."

"I don't know," Fiona said mildly. "She seems to care. She tries pretty hard."

"Oh, I know, Fi. I'm being mean. But don't you think she tries a little *too* hard. Always the big-teeth smile with everything." Sophie mimicked a huge, pained smile. "Why can't she just *relax*?"

"Well, she's new. But yeah," said Fiona, considering. "I guess she is a little —" She opened her eyes wide and made a throttling fist. Sophie snort-laughed.

"Intense? Tightly wound? Rigor mortis-ish? Obviously. But there's something else, something about her that — who does she remind me of?" Sophie frowned, scuffing her boots along the ground, thinking. "Oh! *Yes*. Got it. An optometrist."

"Here we go," said Fiona.

"No, hear me out, Fi. It's like when she's got you in the chair looking through the big goggle-thing, staring at the rows of letters, you know? And she clicks those lenses down and asks, 'Is it clearer with one, or with *two*? With *three* or with four?' And you know *she* knows which lens is better, because she's poked into your optic nerve and stared right straight down into your friggin' brain. So, she's just messing with you. Because it's not *two*, it's one, and it's not *three* (because that was the first choice last time and because she's emphasizing it), it's *four*."

"You're kind of scary, you know that?" murmured Fiona. "You probably need glasses, but you're too busy picking the lens you think she doesn't want you to pick."

"I don't like being messed with," Sophie said.

"Maybe the eye doctor just wants to show you she respects that you know your own eyes, okay?"

"No, Fi. She thinks she knows exactly how my eyes see, and she just wants me to rubber-stamp her diagnosis because I'm technically their owner, the body attached to them. It's *patronizing*, don't you see that?"

"Okay, whatever, enough with the eye doctor analogy," Fiona said wearily, throwing up her hands. She noticed and then minutely examined a small paper cut on the side of her hand.

"At least we've still got Lucy. Thank *God*. Wonder what she thinks of Babs?" Sophie said.

"Does this look infected to you?" Fiona held out her hand.

"What? That there? No, it's just a paper cut. A little one."

"It looks pink. Pinker than a paper cut usually looks." Balancing her backpack on her bent knee, Fiona scrabbled anxiously for her industrial-sized sanitizer.

"It's just a paper cut, Fi."

"It's bleeding a little. Oh, no ..."

"Fi, it'll be fine."

"Look, I have to go and deal with this mess, but I wanted to say it was nice of you to take the part of Abomination. Somehow, it would have been ... weird if Grace had to do that part." Fiona scrubbed her hands with sanitizer. "Ooh, stings."

"I know. That would have been weird. I actually don't think Grace can do *any* part, even Shadowy Friend. I mean, she'd have to move around and say a few lines. She's worse, hey? *Way* worse. Zombie-worse. God knows what they've got her on."

"What's wrong with her? Like, originally, before all the medication. We ever figure that out?" Fiona asked, eyes on the cut, letting her hands dry.

"No." Wayne: Downs, Adnan: autism, Charlie: Tourette's and other things, Fiona: anxiety and OCD. But they'd never been able to pin Grace. And Sophie was conscious that she herself was an impenetrable mystery. "But I guarantee Babs thinks she knows."

Chapter Six

SOPHIE WAS ALONE AT HOME. Her mother was at her night class, her father training for his next half-marathon. His greyhound-lean pack had run by, sleek, competitive older men in expensive spandex, stretching out their hams or hydrating in the pause before he joined them. Her father stumbled down the steps, and the others made a big deal of it, fake falling, slapping him on the back. She watched at the window as they ran off. She saw with a pang of sympathy that her father had a lurching, awkward gait.

Sophronia lurches like a St. John.

Sophie poured out a big glass of red wine and wandered into the drawing room. Some photo albums and scrapbooks had been left on a coffee table. Odd. Her mother and father weren't nostalgic types. She sat on the thick Turkish rug and flipped open a photo album. Little Sophie, solemn, clutching a buck-toothed, ratty stuffed bunny. A formal family portrait, her father slimmer, her mother with longer hair, Sophie looking tear-stained and mutinous.

She took a long sip of wine. Forget the photos. She opened a random scrapbook and a magazine cover stared up at her. Mariam with Hugo, husband number three? Four? Both of them in fringed buckskin jackets, staring straight at the camera in front of that log cabin they lived in for about two months.

To Sophie's parents, Hugo was always "That Fraud." At fifty-three, he'd invented a family history and written a memoir, *Drug Store Indian*, tracing a gut-wrenching and purely fictional history of racial oppression and substance abuse. Mariam had just shaken off a husband and a New York penthouse, and had gone feral in the Rockies to write *A Hundred Wild Horses*, her acclaimed Western-in-reverse. She was ripe for Hugo's literary sensation, his sad blue eyes, graying ponytail, and newly beaded vest. An enterprising reporter interviewed his bewildered relatives and acquaintances in Minneapolis, the hoax was exposed, and Mariam swore off men for a good eight months.

Frauds, the both of you, Sophie thought.

Her phone buzzed. Theo.

just saw a pack of lawyers run by
you alone?

yeah
come over if you want
there's wine!

be right there

Neither of them ever questioned why Theo only ever came over when her parents were out. And why, while she'd been in and out of his house hundreds of times over the years, none of his family had ever been in her house. It was the way things were.

"Your parents are okay, Ronny," Theo had said once, hunting for the right words to explain it, "but they're kind of ... chilly. Uptight. Leetle bit snobby, maybe?"

"A lot snobby. Don't worry Theo, believe me, I know." She would never tell him how her parents talked about Theo's family's small bungalow. "That House on the Corner" had too many children (always an exaggerated number; eight or ten or twelve. They had five), its roof needed repairing, its bushes were untrimmed, its lawn haphazardly mown. Mr. Silva read in an easy chair kept on the front porch. "A little peace and quiet," he'd explained to Sophie once in his weary, quiet voice. But for Sophie's parents, furniture in the front yard signaled a frat house or worse.

The Silva house was also, Sophie thought but could never express, everything her own house was not: warm, comfortable, lived-in, casual, filled with people and life and love.

Sophie had wondered in that moment what Mr. and Mrs. Silva thought of her parents, of her family, of their house. *They were too nice to bitch about us or laugh at us,* she thought, *but did they raise an eyebrow at the ongoing renovations or the putting-green lawn? Or did they not even notice us at all?*

There was a tap on the back door. Always the back.

As usual, Theo came in talking.

"So, I saved you a piece of cake. Just a hunk, but I practically had to fight Anthony for it. Kid's getting *strong*. It's pretty good, got this little layer of jam in it. Some client of Mom's got her this little cake, like, only this big." He held out his hands in a circle. "Who makes a cake only that big? Like, technically for one person? Mom just slapped a bunch of forks on the counter, and we attacked the thing. Anyway, that's why it's shaped a bit weird."

Mrs. Silva, a stylist, would run her hands through Sophie's thick hair and murmur "so thick, so springy, so much body — I have clients that would kill for this hair." Mrs. Silva, who had winced as if in pain when Sophie described her mom's maroon pixie cut.

"Thanks, Theo," said Sophie, eating the piece with her fingers. "Mmm, that's incredible. Want some wine?" She swung around to grab the bottle, but Theo beat her to it.

"I got it, I got it, Ronny. No offense, but you always end up spilling half of it."

"Hardly *half*, but I know. But have you noticed I'm usually *less* clumsy when I'm drinking?" Sophie loved that Theo called her "Ronny." Technically his abbreviation of Soph*ro*nia, but mostly it was just a stupid nickname. Better than "Blob" and "Blobber," his nicknames for his twelve-year-old twin siblings, Daria and Edward.

"Yeah, that's true. Wonder why? Just more chill when you're tanked or what? Because you do get chill."

"And you talk. Even more than usual."

"I know," said Theo, helping himself to a glass of wine and sitting on the floor with her. Nick ran down the stairs at the sound of Theo's voice, and settled in his lap. "Maybe that's why we get along — you're too chill to get away from me talking, and so I have somebody to talk *at*. It's perfect. Why didn't we ever get together?"

She looked at him quickly, but he was just smiling and looking down at the pictures.

"Aww, there's baby Ronny. Damn, you were *cute*! What happened?"

She smacked his shoulder, leaving her hand on his back as she pretended to look at the picture.

"We never got together because you were always interested in some other girl. *Lots* of other girls." She tried to keep her voice light.

"Not *always*," he said. "Ronny —" Their eyes met, and the room suddenly seemed quiet, hushed. Sophie's heart knocked. "But it was always Calvin for you, right? Story of my life."

"Not *always*," she said as Nick jumped off his lap. "But maybe we're better as friends, right? I mean we get along great, but in rom-coms it's pretty much mandatory to hate the person first. Or do you think we —" She gestured sharply and smacked her elbow into the coffee table.

"*Shit, funny bone*," she said, wincing and laughing as he tried to grab her elbow to rub it. *Shit, moment passed.*

"Look at this one," he said, back to the pictures, "you beside a growth chart. Man, tall kid! Up, up! On your feet, soldier. Back-to-back!"

"Exactly the same height," she pointed out when they were standing. "We're both five-ten. How many times do we have to do this?"

"Are you *serious*? I'm practically an inch taller now! Maybe a little more." He felt their heads with the flat of his hand.

They measured hands and feet against each other's, laughed at photos, and finished off the bottle of wine.

"What's everyone else doing?" she asked casually.

"You mean what's *Calvin* doing," Theo said.

"No, just everyone," she lied. "The general population."

But she had been thinking about his older brother. She'd had a crush on Calvin for years. Pretty much everybody had. He wasn't just good-looking. He was beautiful. He was so beautiful Sophie found it hard to look at him, for fear she'd forget what was going on around her, forget what she was saying, and just stare help-lessly. It was hard to imagine how Mr. and Mrs. Silva had even produced someone so beautiful — tall, broad shoulders, beautiful cheekbones, perfect teeth, thick eyelashes.

Theo had the same coloring, the same thick eyelashes, but a

crooked nose, a huge smile, a sprinkling of acne. Fun, kind, wicked-sarcastic sense of humor; she'd had to remind Theo of all his good qualities repeatedly during his years of unrequited crushes and failed relationships. At least he'd *had* crushes and relationships. She'd never even had an actual conversation with Calvin.

"Okay, what's Calvin doing?" She knew he was dating Tamara Stepchuk from her school. She collected any scrap of information on him like a spy.

"Basketball, probably. Forget him. You got *this* right in front of you," Theo gestured ironically up and down his thin body, at his rumpled T-shirt and baggy sweatpants, "and you can think of another man? What the hell is *wrong* with you?"

Sophie laughed. Theo always made her laugh. He could laugh at himself, at her, at her family, at his family, at the world. It was so liberating. The Gayle-St. Johns took themselves very, very seriously. There were small, bitter, or cynical smiles. There were shots at other people's expense, often couched in literary terms. But laughter, genuine laughter, was very rare.

"I'm waiting for a text from Lauren," Theo said. "Remember, that new girl I told you about? Don't want to jinx it, but ..." Theo sighed. "So anyway, I hear your granny is in town. The Great Lady. Queen Bitch. Saw her on the news at some conference. This her too?" Theo pointed to the news clipping, leaning in to have a look at it. "Skinny little thing to have given you and your mom so much shit."

Sophie laughed again. Mariam *was* a skinny little thing.

"Sometimes it's the little ones you have to look out for. They can be mean. Oh, God, I haven't told you. Babs told us we're putting on Mariam's play. Remember *Abomination*?"

"Was that the one I had to read in grade ten? About that sad kid with no face? Man, I *hated* that story. Everybody was so *mean*. And what's up with the flying?"

"Yeah. Well, there's a play version and our class is doing it. I think Babs just desperately wants to meet Mariam. Anyway, it's going to be so very lame, which absolutely delights me. Downside is that we're doing it in front of people. Parents."

"*Your* parents? Granny?"

Sophie snorted a bit of wine out her nose.

"Absolutely, most definitely, not. No way in hell they're hearing about it. I meant the other parents." An image of Wayne's nice family who watched hockey together flicked through her mind. Fiona's pale younger brother, Fiona's mom, who always seemed stressed but who asked how you were. Adnan's gentle, kind parents, his mother wearing a colorful sari. Grace? Nobody knew which relative she was living with now.

"What role do you have anyway? No, please, just tell me it's not —"

"Abomination!" they said at the same time.

"Jeez," laughed Theo, delighted. "Well, good luck with that. How're you going to do the faceless face shit?"

"I don't know. Nylon over my head? Fencing mask?"

"Fencing mask! Yes! Way cooler. Badass. The nylon would be, just, *brrrr* — creepy."

"And mitts."

"Right, no fingers. Man, *such* a stupid story." He shook his head.

"I can't even begin to describe how Mariam would trash our performance if she ever saw it," said Sophie. "She can be so vicious; you have no idea."

Theo cocked his head to one side.

"Why do you guys let her have so much power over you? When she says some mean shit, why can't you all be, like, 'hey, Mariam, fuck right off!'"

Sophie stared at him in admiration. To even *think* of saying that. To Mariam.

"I love you, Theo."

"Yeah, yeah, I know you do, Ronny. I love you, too." His phone buzzed as he said it.

"Lauren," he said.

"Oh good," she said. *God damn you, Lauren.*

"Deep breath," he said. "Wish me luck."

"Good luck," she said automatically. "Just be *yourself*, Theo," she said earnestly.

"Yeah, that's worked out *great* for me so far."

"Then just be someone *else*, Theo," she said earnestly.

He barked out a laugh, ruffled her hair, and sprinted to the back door.

Chapter Seven

"*ABOOOOOMINATION!*" WAYNE BELLOWED IN A monster-truck voice, throwing out his arm. Fiona's flinch just saved her from being smacked in the head.

"Stay or leave, but make your choice," Lucy whispered the line.

"Stay awaaaay! And make … make …"

"Nonsense, it is all nonsense," Adnan interjected his line in a quick monotone.

"Whoops, just let Wayne-God finish there, buddy," said Lucy.

"Stay awaaaay! Stay awaaaay!" Wayne roared, grinning.

Grace totally missed her cue for Shadowy Friend, only turning her head in a very careful way when Lucy touched her shoulder.

Ms. Linden watched, crouched on a stool, a muscle clenching in her jaw. Sophie saw her flip quickly through the script, then set it down on the floor.

"Babs!" Sophie said, pulling up a stool.

"What? Oh, haha, for Barbara you mean?"

"Yeah, you don't mind me calling you *Babs*, do you? I think it would help me connect." Sophie looked at her earnestly. "Integrate, you know?" She clasped her hands together, linking the fingers tightly. *Let's see if you have any kind of shit-detector like I do, Babs.*

"Oh, absolutely, absolutely." Ms. Linden smiled. "But you know what I think, Sophie?" She leaned in confidentially. "I think you're just messing with me. But if it means you'll talk to me, 'Babs' away!"

Sophie blinked at her, unprepared for that.

Ms. Linden ran a bony hand through her hair.

"Tell me what you think about this, Sophie. I was wondering if we should change the format of the play somewhat. Don't get me wrong: everyone is doing a great job and the rehearsals are going, ah, really well."

Liar, thought Sophie.

"I'm absolutely *loving* them," Sophie said enthusiastically, truthfully. She was thoroughly enjoying the Opportunity Class's abysmal butchering of Mariam's story.

"Excellent! Excellent. I'm glad to hear you're enjoying this. Well, what better material could we have to work with?"

Doesn't it bother you that you're so transparent, Babs? You are so desperate to talk about Mariam. All these hints you keep dropping, that this work is a classic, a masterpiece. Brightly looking at me like I'm supposed to be all grateful and humble to be related to Mariam. You have no idea how done I am with all that.

"That's so true. Wayne, Fiona, the whole gang. Great group." Sophie wondered if her smile looked as fake as it felt.

Ms. Linden nodded vigorously. Guiltily, Sophie thought.

"*Wonderful* group. Just amazing students we have in this Room 107 family." She paused. "And also, of course, the play! Your grandmother's work! So powerful. Such an affirmation of the strength of the human *spirit*. What a brilliant mind she must have."

Sophie looked down, picked at a hangnail.

"But what I'm seeing," Ms. Linden went on, "is that some of the kids are finding learning their lines ... difficult. Stressful."

She looked over at Grace, who was staring dully at the ground. "And that's about the last thing we want, right? That's hardly therapeutic."

"Stay awaaaaay!" Wayne bellowed in the background. There was a burst of laughter.

"Wayne doesn't sound stressed," said Sophie.

Ms. Linden laughed and threw Wayne a fond look. *She genuinely likes all of us*, Sophie thought, *even me*.

"No, Wayne's having the time of his life," Ms. Linden said with disconcerting honesty. "Still, the lines are a problem. So, what I was thinking is that I could narrate the play, describe the action, and the characters could silently act it out! *Tableaus*, if you see what I mean. Maybe a spotlight! Dramatic. Minimalist. It could be a really unique way of telling the story and could be just as powerful. More so, even! And it might make the play more manageable, more accessible."

It might make it look less of a disaster, you mean, thought Sophie. It was hard not to be cynical.

"After all," said Ms. Linden, "we have an obligation to really do *justice* to this phenomenal story." She gripped her hands together, like justice was there, throttled tight in her fists.

All of a sudden, Sophie felt weary, old. Another follower, another Mariam-worshipper. *Abomination* was usually discussed so solemnly, in such sacred tones that it made her want to throw something.

The wanting to throw something had actually become an increasing problem. Because recently she'd actually started throwing things. Small things at first. An eraser at that asshole Corbin McTavish in Math. Pelted him hard in the temple. That one felt right, even *just*. He'd mimicked her stiff-legged gait one day, one bad day, with full-on Frankenstein monster parody.

Then she'd thrown a marker at her mother when she criticized that class project on the stages of rock erosion, but again, could she help her hands being so clumsy that staying in the lines was a total ordeal? The piece of lasagna she'd thrown at her father was also richly deserved. Righteous lasagna. Yet again, he had talked about the Silvas like they were dirt. "That mess of a house on the corner with the ten kids." She'd shown him mess.

But the missiles were getting bigger. Her Doc Martens boot. That one was a mistake. She'd aimed for Louis (who had just mocked nice foreign student Jane Choy's accent) and connected, but the boot bounced off his shoulder and hit Chloe in the face. She felt bad about Chloe, but was it her fault that Chloe was basically a hemophiliac and bled from her nose forever? Was it her fault that Louis was a total racist jerk who started it all? That stupid boot-throwing started the unraveling. She got suspended (but was proud of the fact that she took Louis down with her). The suspension led to those awful anger-management therapy sessions, check-ins with the student safety officer.

And it all led to her being put in the Opportunity Class with all the other problem cases. And somehow her throwing didn't end there.

The chair she'd thrown at Mr. Green in advanced English last semester was her hall-of-famer. And that one was all Mariam's fault. It was during an analysis of "The Path through the Sea," one of her short stories. Mr. Green wasn't one of Mariam's sycophants. He fell into the other camp: Mariam's bitter skeptics. Mariam called them her "sad and squalid little enemies," and there were a lot of them. Critics, fellow writers, reviewers. Even high school English teachers.

Mr. Green had assured the class right off the bat that Mariam Gayle's work was "predictable, infantile, florid, and vastly, vastly overrated." He would have been astounded to hear that Sophie agreed with him.

He had spent the entire year needling and baiting Mariam's granddaughter in a one-sided, pathetic battle. He called on her repeatedly, read paragraphs from her essays out loud, criticized her openly, and fished for any information about Mariam. And Sophie was trapped, unable to predict when it was coming, when he would single her out. It was a year of torture, a year of being the target-fish in the barrel. He knew it, she knew it, the whole class must have known it.

That day in December, the chair-throwing day, Mr. Green had sat, his scrawny haunch propped on the side of a desk, his thin, intense face avid behind his thick glasses.

"Sophie," he said, bypassing a few raised hands, "let's hear something from you. To what do you think your illustrious grandmama's metaphor of the sea in this story refers? It's unoriginal, hardly at the epic level of Hemingway or Melville, but surely someone of your dear old gran's mythic stature meant *something* by it."

She stared at him, deliberately keeping her face blank. He sometimes lost interest if she gave him no reaction. Not today. He'd probably calculated that he had less than a month left of class to get a reaction from her. A winter break yawning in front of him without his daily fix of sadism.

"No opinions?" He stroked his scrappy beard, let the silence lengthen. "Not even a guess?" He wandered up and down the aisle, elaborate in his casualness. Then he turned back to the attack. "Not one, Sophie? Come, come — reach deep into those formidable

Gayle genes of yours. Think about this phe*nom*enal piece of literature we have just read. The sea. A metaphor. For what?" These
last words he enunciated clearly, snapped them out crisply as if
she was someone who didn't speak the language.

"Maybe society?" hazarded a girl near Sophie. "Like, a sea of
people."

"Or civilization? History?" said another student.

Mr. Green silenced them by holding up a hand, and regarded
Sophie with a very faint smile, his eyes dancing. Sophie stared
back, poker-faced, not giving an inch.

"Maybe she actually meant the sea," said one of the girls who'd
turned around to watch. "Maybe there's no metaphor at all."
Mr. Green gave her the hand.

A boy's voice from the back of the room broke the lengthen-
ing silence.

"Look, do you actually want an answer or not?"

"Ah, a diversionary attempt!" Mr. Green strolled to the back
of the class. "Very gallant, Tomas. But I think Sophie is a big girl
who can speak for herself. Hmmm, Sophie?" He'd wandered back
up to the front of the class, resuming his haunch-on-the-desk pose.
He had the book (*Selected Works in World Short Fiction*) clasped
open on his chest, anchored with both hands, like a shield.

He's loving this, she thought. He's loving torturing Mariam
Gayle's sixteen-year-old granddaughter in front of the whole
class. How pathetic is that? What did he gain from this? Was he a
frustrated writer? Did he have a sad and squalid life?

She would not look away. She would not give him that. *Look
out, Mr. Green, I've faced worse than you.*

The silence lengthened excruciatingly.

The class waited, watched, the tension in the room escalated.

"Sophie? We have all the time in the world, you know. We can wait. And none of you are leaving until I get some kind of answer. From Sophie. Some nugget of pure and shining wisdom from the illustrious Gayle lineage."

Sophie calmly let the silence stretch.

Finally, Mr. Green gave an elaborate, triumphant shrug of his tiny shoulders.

"Disappointing, so disappointing," he murmured as though to himself, but loud enough that everyone could hear. He turned away.

It was only then that Sophie spoke.

"Hey, Damien." She'd looked up his first name for just this moment. Damien, devil. Easy to remember. She forced her voice to sound casual, conversational. "I've been wondering all year: have you got some kind of obscene crush on my grandma?" A ripple of shocked giggles in the class. "She's way older than you, but I'm guessing you're not picky. Disappointing. So disappointing, Damien. And pathetic. Totally. Fucking. Pathetic." She bit the last words out like he had before when he'd been goading her, enunciating clearly.

Mr. Green was clearly taken aback by the ferocity of the reaction he'd been prompting all year. He tried to laugh in an ironic way.

"Ah, Ms. Gayle-St. John lives! She speaks! I was beginning —"

But Sophie was just warming up, and she cut him off.

"— and I don't actually teach high school English, *Damien*, so I'm no stellar English *scholar* like yourself," — she let the words drip with sarcasm — "but knowing my dear old gran, I'd guess the sea is a metaphor for booze."

The class laughed. Mr. Green looked down at the book in his

hands, flipping the pages with elaborate unconcern. *Trying to think up some pithy retort,* Sophie thought, her face hot from the attention. She didn't care what they thought. She didn't care about any of them. Mr. Green looked around at the class.

"Interesting, isn't it, ladies and gentlemen, how genetics work. Sophie seems to have inherited the great lady's famed rudeness. She thinks she's different, but she's *just* like her grandmother …"

She had leapt to her feet and thrown her chair before she even realized what she was going to do. And when, in horror, in slow motion, she saw her hands let it go, she yelled, "DUCK!"

Mr. Green leapt to the side in an ungainly lurch, like an unathletic kid in a dodgeball game, the one who lurked nervously at the back. He crashed down awkwardly, a tangled mess of arms and legs and paper, his glasses flying off and spinning into the corner. The chair ricocheted off the wall behind him.

Sophie stifled a hysterical giggle as Shea Turner turned to offer a huge smile and a high five, but already the adrenaline was ebbing.

Mrs. Boychuk, the teacher in the next room, the one sharing the wall that the chair hit, rushed in and hauled Mr. Green to his feet. Without his glasses, his eyes looked weak and vulnerable, moist and pink. A nocturnal animal squinting in the sunshine. It was like seeing him as a newborn baby, or worse, seeing him naked.

Sophie slid to the ground, back against the wall, hiding her head in her arms.

"Everyone out! Out. Just leave her and get out," Mrs. Boychuk ordered, heading into full lockdown mode. "NOW!" In a fire-drill atmosphere humming with suppressed excitement, the English class gathered up their things and filed out.

A girl from the back of the class stopped by Sophie as she walked out.

"You okay?" she asked. "He's such a jerk."

Sophie didn't lift her head. She heard her sigh and move away, and quietly say to the teacher at the door, "Mr. Green deserved it. He's bullied her all year."

"And she *did* yell 'duck,'" added Shea excitedly. "Didn't have to do that. Could've just let him have it. Which I would have actually preferred …"

Sophie, her head in her hands, was touched that two of her classmates, neither of whom she'd ever spoken to, had come to her defense. She thought about how she'd sat in this class all year, hating it and everything about it, and regretted that maybe she could have made some friends.

"There is absolutely no excuse …"

She heard a muffled, impromptu teacher conference in the hall, mention of calling the police. *Oh God,* thought Sophie wearily, *if they only knew how tired I feel. I couldn't be less of a threat now.*

Then she heard Lucy's voice.

"Oh, for Christ's sake," she heard Lucy say clearly. "You can't be serious. The cops? That is ridiculous."

Lucy, the Opportunity Class aide, had only started a few months ago. But she took charge like a pro. She got rid of the gawkers, came into the room, shut the door, righted the chair, dragged it over beside Sophie, and straddled it backwards. Her round face was calm, a rueful smile tugging at her mouth.

"So. Why the fuck d'you do a stupid thing like that, Sophie?" she'd asked conversationally.

Sophie's hostility had evaporated, and she'd given a sob-laugh at Lucy's honesty. *Thank you. It was stupid. If he hadn't said I was just like Mariam …*

No one had ever, not once, asked her why she did these things. They just talked about the anger. Nobody asked *why* the anger. Nobody knew about the mocking, the prodding, the endless taunting. Nobody knew about the thick, black rage that washed over her, obscuring her vision and leaving her exhausted, frightened, and spent. They just piled on after it happened, suspending her, modifying their behavior management strategies, having meetings, calling her parents. It was all so tediously predictable.

Right now, slumped against the wall, black eyeliner smeared by the angry scrubbing away of tears, she just wanted to die.

Her worst, most secret fear was not that she was crazy or even that she was a screwup. It was that, in some strange and pathetic way, she needed the drama of these outbursts. Her very worst fear was Mr. Green's ill-fated suggestion: that she was just like Mariam.

"The fuck do *you* care?"

"I'm interested. Just interested."

As the silence dragged on, Lucy talked. She told Sophie that high school was sometimes hard. She'd had an eating disorder "for, like, forever," exacerbated by the accidental death of her cousin by a drunk driver. Lucy told her that one of her boys, a good kid, was going through a really rough patch in grade five, and they were considering changing schools. She told her why she'd transferred from her last school, because of the "power-shit" from the teacher she'd been paired with.

And Sophie listened and calmed down. And, looking desperately at Lucy's round face, under its scrappy, dyed-blond hair, somehow it all poured out. She'd told Lucy more that afternoon than she'd told eleven years of doctors, counselors, teachers, and psychiatrists.

She told her about not remembering things she used to remember. She told her about her marks tanking even though she'd always thought she was smart. She told her about her stiff legs and her clumsy hands and her rage and her secret drinking and her hatred and her fear. She told Lucy some of it, at least. She herself didn't know all of it. It was like sitting at a window on a fast train — you saw just a glimpse of peoples' lives. A little boy holding his mother's hand, his lit-up face turned to tell her something, then gone. A man turning his head to glare at the person who bumped his shoulder, then gone. A hunched old man in a hat walking a scruffy dog on a red leash, then gone. Only, the split-second glimpses Sophie got were of herself.

Anyway, Lucy had never, ever, not once, used anything she said against her afterwards. As far as she trusted anybody, she trusted Lucy.

"Good talk, Sophie," Lucy had said finally, slapping her thigh, like they'd been figuring out where to go for lunch.

"Whatever."

"And hey, you know the chair-throwing? Not gonna happen again," Lucy predicted.

Sophie eyed her. "How do you know?"

"Because I'll rip off your arm and slap you with the wet end," she said. She lunged in, miming the action, twisting Sophie's arm. Sophie had barked out a surprised, watery hiccup of a laugh and it was all over.

At least this day, this crisis, was over.

Chapter Eight

THE CLASS WAS PAINTING SETS for the play. Ms. Linden had convinced the caretaker to drag in the huge sheets of cardboard from the new gym equipment. They had propped them on top of old bedsheets lining the floor.

Sophie was relieved to see that Grace was painting, participating. Although when she looked closer, she saw her moving the brush side to side automatically in exactly the same arc, creating a dark, muddy swath. A mud-brown rainbow.

"This is *your* play, my friends. The background sets can be as impressionistic as you'd like. *Beautiful!*" Ms. Linden was ecstatic, either because everyone was participating or because nobody was having a meltdown. Room 107 was actually peaceful this morning.

She darted here and there, peppering them with suggestions.

"So, it might be good to have a 'lowering sky' like the play mentions. Which means dark and oppressive. And perhaps a shaft of sunlight for when Abomination flies. Maybe over here? With a diagonal slant to the sunlight?"

"I thought this was *our* play, my *friends*," Sophie muttered to Fiona, who was wearing gloves and painting a tiny area in grays and blues. "And I've been meaning to ask how we're going to do that whole flying thing," said Sophie. "It's pretty integral to the plot. I mean, Abomination actually *flies*. It'd be pathetic if I just walked offstage when the whole point is that I'm supposed to be soaring into the sky."

"Yeah, good point. Ask." Fiona wasn't really listening.

"So," Sophie said, raising her voice, "how are we doing the part in the play where Abomination flies?"

"Well, symbolically —" Ms. Linden began.

"— it's not symbolic," interrupted Sophie. "And it's pretty clear it's not just a little hop. It's a full-on, up-into-the-clouds flight. So how are we supposed to do that?"

"Well, I thought sym*bol*ically —"

"— because you'd have to have ropes and pulleys and beams and things if I'm actually supposed to fly."

"I want to fly!" roared Wayne. "I'm God! God can fly, too!" Adnan started to flap his hands.

Ms. Linden clapped her hands sharply three times like a kindergarten teacher calling the class to order.

"Given the technical constraints of this room, which is not a proper *theater*," Ms. Linden said, "we obviously can't approximate actual *flight*. Not possible. Wayne, will you please not jump like that? Paint, *paint*! No flying. No, nobody is flying. So," she said, turning to Sophie, "we have to do something different. More stylized. I thought perhaps Abomination could do something like this."

Ms. Linden spread her arms, poked out her neck, and executed some long, awkward leaps. She looked like an ungainly bird, one of the long-legged ones that stands in the shallows to feed and cumbersomely takes to the air in struggling leaps and bounds.

"Okay, no way in hell I'm doing *that*," said Sophie, crossing her arms. "Noooo way." That sort of thing was exactly what she'd been fearing. Looking like a fool in front of everyone.

"You don't need to be rude, Sophie," Ms. Linden said, a little out of breath from her exertions. "I'd love to hear *your* suggestions."

Lucy, who had been inching Grace to another spot on the cardboard, looked over.

"What about that old projector cart in the closet? Think you could lie on your stomach on that and we give you a shove?"

"*I* want a ride on the cart!" yelled Wayne, who'd been leaping clumsily like Ms. Linden, and crash-landed into Sophie.

"Wayne, enough! *Jeez!*" Sophie snapped. "Sorry, buddy, but you smeared my shirt." She turned to Lucy. "That might actually work, Lucy. Abomination's flight is supposed to be smooth. She's supposed to *glide*."

"'Gliding, soaring, the wind smoothly caressing her smooth, faceless face, calm, calm, calm,'" Ms. Linden quoted excitedly. Sophie ground her teeth. Babs quoted the stupid book at any opportunity.

"Sure, whatever," she said.

"And we could wave blue material in front of the cart to represent the sky," said Ms. Linden, warming to the idea. "So, all the audience would see is Abomination, gliding! Brilliant!" Sophie had to admire her enthusiasm. "Lucy, high five!"

Lucy held up her hand in a good-natured way.

And Ms. Linden fumbled around in the storage closet to find the projector cart.

Chapter Nine

SOPHIE SLID DOWN THE SLIDE into the Silvas' basement and landed, as usual, in an ungainly heap at the bottom on the floor. It had led to her first nickname with the Silva boys: Crash.

"Why can't you *ever* do that right?" said Daria, who swooped down gracefully, landed on her feet, and barely paused to leap into the room.

"We can't all be friggin' twelve-year-old gymnasts," said Sophie, rubbing her knees. "And would it kill you people to have a pillow at the bottom? Some kind of cushioning? For guests?"

"*Dancers*. I'm not a gymnast. I dance."

"You know what I mean. Plus, you also have practice." She looked around. "Where are the boys?" There were usually a few Silva boys lounging on the couches, playing video games or watching sports. She'd hoped for a glimpse of Calvin.

"No idea." Daria was peering into the ice-encrusted freezer. "Mom said there was some ice cream in here somewhere."

Sophie wandered over to the far corner of the basement, where the boys slept. Bookshelves separated off the four twin mattresses from the TV room. On one side, Calvin and Theo, the older boys. On the other side, Anthony and Edward, the younger ones. Daria, the only girl, got the second bedroom upstairs all to herself. Sophie had always been fascinated by this boy-basement, this gaming man cave. To an only child, it looked wonderful, like a perpetual sleepover. It wasn't, apparently. Sophie had heard endless bitching from Theo about the Silvas' basement arrangements.

"Calvin snores. Like, bad. Like: *RRRRrrrr-RRRHHHHH*," he mimicked. "And he uses so much body spray, we're all probably getting lung cancer from breathing it in all the time. *And* he takes up all the space with his clothes. But Anthony does this creepy, deep-voiced, death-muttering in his sleep. And sometimes, totally asleep, he *walks around*. Which would just freak you right out, Ronny, because he doesn't even answer if you say, 'Anthony, you okay? Go back to bed.' Eddie's not bad, the best of the bunch. Quiet. But it's the video games. That kid's always, always got that TV locked up."

Sophie peeked into Calvin and Theo's side. She breathed deeply the smell of Calvin's body spray, wanted to touch the mess of sheets and blankets on his bed, smooth his pillow. She smiled to herself at the thought of Calvin getting ready in this cramped mess, and coming out every day looking like some exotic, gorgeous male model.

"Found it, Ronny!" Daria was holding up a bucket of ice cream. "Not even freezer-burnt. Much anyway. Come *on*. Let's go."

They climbed the stairs up to the kitchen just as the kitchen door banged open. Calvin came in, casually, freakishly, devastatingly handsome. Sophie froze and her mouth dried up.

"Hey, you," she said, tilting her head to look up at him with what she hoped was a normal smile.

"Hey, Blobber, hey, Ronny." He was preoccupied, barely looked at them. "I'm *starving*. Any of that pizza left from last night?"

"Nope," said Daria, chipping away at the ice cream. "You ate most of it anyway."

Alison Hughes

"Want me to order one?" Sophie asked, taking out her phone.

Calvin looked right at her, flashed her a smile, and her heart did a fish-flop.

"Thanks, Ronny, but I gotta go. Just came home to dump my backpack and get my jersey." He grabbed an apple and a granola bar, and she heard the *whoosh* as he slid into the basement. No clatter at the bottom.

"So, Daria," said Sophie, wrenching her attention away from the basement. "What's up?" Daria had practically tackled her when she was walking home, saying she needed to vent, needed some "girl-time."

As Daria poured out her seventh-grade angst, a litany of mean-girl innuendos and boy problems, Sophie sat and listened, a sympathetic look on her face, an ear to the basement.

Chapter Ten

"BUT FI, YOU HAVE TO admit, it was way out of line," Sophie said. "Old Babs there *bringing in* Epiphany Tree. We all know the play, we *knew* we'd have to have the tree in there, but she didn't trust us to make it. 'Oh, we're all such a *family*, so wonderful, such lovely souls, but I'll be doing the serious shit because I can't trust you losers with it.'"

"She didn't say *anything* like that," said Fiona. "She just made the stupid Epiphany Tree because she did. It wasn't some kind of statement. We needed a tree. She made one. It's pretty, actually. Abomination has to fly from there or near there or something, right?"

"Yeah, we all *knew* that —"

"Then why didn't you say something? Why didn't *you* make it? You just want this whole play to tank, don't you?" Fiona said, rounding on Sophie. "You want it to look stupid and amateurish and lame because you get some kind of twisted satisfaction from that. You hate the story, you hate your grandmother, so you want to wreck it."

Sophie stopped in the middle of the sidewalk. Fiona didn't stop, so Sophie stumbled after her.

"Fi! I can't believe you're saying this." She deflected Fiona's truth with defensive anger. "I'm the one standing up for our class."

"Are you, Sophie? Really? Doesn't seem like that to me. It seems like you want the play to be a disaster. And you know what? You're dragging all of us down with you. Is that standing up for us?"

"Fi, Babs *made the tree*. We were supposed to do everything. I mean, it was nice of her to help, but maybe it means she doesn't trust us."

"Maybe not. But neither do you."

IN HER ROOM, SOPHIE TOOK out the invitations to the play Ms. Linden had handed out. She'd used stock "You're Invited!" cards, but had written the names and the date and time of the play in calligraphy. Those creepy smiling/frowning theater faces adorned the cards.

"And here's your parents' invitation, Sophie," Ms. Linden had said. She half turned away, then turned back, elaborately casual, flicking through the cards. "Oh, almost forgot this one. For your grandmother if she'd care to join us. I heard her interview today, so if she's still in town next Wednesday, we'd be honored to have her." Sophie snatched the invitation and shoved it in her backpack.

Sophie rummaged in her closet, looking for the ashtray she'd made in shop class in grade seven, a lumpy snarl of metal that weighed about five pounds. She'd used it maybe three times, when she thought she might be cooler if she started smoking, then chucked it to the back of her closet when she found she couldn't do it without coughing uncontrollably. No long, cool inhale for her — just hacking and wheezing and eye-watering. But the ashtray had come in handy when she'd needed to burn things over the years. Things she couldn't bear to think of other people reading if for some reason she died during the day. Excruciating journal pages, toe-curling, pompous early essays where she'd misused every big word her parents dropped. That crushing note from Cameron Winter in grade five: "I only like you as a freind." All torn up in little pieces, all burnt.

It took a while for her shaky hands to shred the invitation to her parents, dropping the thin, curling strips into the ashtray. Then she shredded Mariam's. She finally got a match lit and torched them both.

She knew she could have just chucked them in a garbage can on the way home instead of being such a drama queen, sitting here in the dark, watching them burn. But there was something satisfying about fire. Something final. She watched the invitations burn to charred rubble, fanning away the smoke so that the fire detectors didn't start shrieking.

Mariam Gayle — it figured that those were the last two words to burn.

Chapter Eleven

"I'M STUDYING AT FIONA'S LATER, just so you know," Sophie said on the next Wednesday as she cleaned up after dinner. Lie. It was the night of the play, but she wasn't telling her mother that.

"Oh? What are you studying?" asked her mother, barely looking up from a paper she was marking. For a second, Sophie blanked out. She hadn't expected any follow-up questions, any interest at all.

"Legal Studies. Test in a few days." Lie. They'd already had the test.

Silence.

"Well, if you need a ride ..." Her mother looked up suddenly, her eyes huge behind her thick glasses.

"Nope, I'm good."

"Sophie. Please. I hate that phrase. 'I'm good.' The only phrase I detest more is 'It's all good.' I just read that in a student *essay*, if you can believe that. Rubbishy pseudo-psychological cant. What can it possibly mean? What is 'It'? And 'all good'? How can every-thing be *all* good?"

"Ooookay," Sophie sighed. "Down, girl. It's just something people say." Her mother carried on as if she hadn't spoken.

"Another one that makes me wild is using 'literally' for some-thing one wants to emphasize, rather than correctly, as something that must be exactly, precisely the case. And honestly, some of these students *text* rather than *write*. I had a 'wanna' a few essays ago. 'Wanna.' Seriously." Her mother shook her head, pursed her lips, and wrote a long comment on the essay she was marking.

Sophie looked at her mother's bent head and wondered what she was like as a teacher. As a professor. *Please God, don't let her be like Mr. Green. Would she be like that? Bitter and twisted and conscious of the class's contempt? Compensating by ridiculing and demeaning her students?*

She'd once looked her up on Rate My Prof, and the comments from the undergrads made her toes curl. Sophie remembered "pompous," "hyper-critical," "scathing," and "elitist." She also remembered one that advised other students: "Unless you're Charles Dickens, do not, repeat NOT, take a course from Prof. Gayle-St. John. Life is *way* too short." Sophie had never looked again.

"So, what are you doing tonight, Mom?"

Her mother grimaced and indicated the pile of papers in front of her. She glanced at the clock.

"Dad should be here soon. And Mariam said she might pop by for a drink after her meeting with the university chancellor and board of governors. They're naming a building after her."

Of course they were. Suddenly, Sophie found the house unbearable. Oppressive. She needed air.

"Well, have fun with that," she said. "I gotta go."

THIS ACTUALLY DOESN'T LOOK THAT *bad*, thought Sophie, looking around Room 107. Somehow, they'd managed to capture the claustrophobic, eerie atmosphere of *Abomination*. The sets were bleak, streaks of deep blues and grays and Grace's scrubbed black patches. But those felt right. That could be a lowering, turbulent sky. If you squinted a little, that patch could be the sea.

They'd covered the room lights with dark sheets, casting dim shadows over the front of the class where they were to perform. Epiphany Tree teetered in its pot, clearly a fake Christmas tree, but wound with sparkly gauze that glittered softly in the gloom.

"Spooky in here," said Fiona with a shiver, pulling the folds of her costume closer. "I can't *wait* until this is over. Why do we even have to do this?"

Sophie was just glad Fiona was talking to her. There had been a few days of frosty politeness between them, broken by Sophie asking to help feed Morton.

"I have no idea, Fi. Let's just try to get through it. And get everyone else through it. Where's Grace?"

Fiona nodded over to a dark corner. Ms. Linden had her arm around Grace, murmuring to her. *You never give up, do you, Babs? You really care.*

"Heeeeeere's God!" said Wayne, strutting into the room happily. He was wearing a dark-blue bathrobe over his clothes. It trailed on the ground and the sleeves covered his hands. He and Lucy had fashioned a kind of halo out of aluminum foil, and it sat askew on his brown hair.

"Looking good, God!" said Sophie, raising her hand for his high five.

Adnan was the last to arrive, jittering and flapping his way into the class.

"Nonsense it is all nonsense it is all nonsense …"

This is so ridiculously stressful for him, Sophie thought, hearing a hum of people talking outside in the hall. *She* was nervous.

Just imagine how someone like Adnan must feel, someone who needed structure and routine so desperately. And Fiona seemed rattled. And maybe even Grace was feeling something. *Wayne is the most well-adjusted of all of us*, she thought.

Ms. Linden swept over, bringing with her an atmosphere of intensity and nervousness and excitement. She grinned at them and pushed up her glasses with that middle finger. She was wearing a confusing, bizarre costume — a long, flowing dress with an elaborately embroidered Chinese shawl wrapped around her bony shoulders. She'd pinned fake roses to the side of a hairband, and they were sliding it heavily to the right. Sophie stared at her for a minute. *Is this just how Babs dresses up? Why on earth would she …* Then she remembered the famous line from *Abomination*, referencing a long-dead matriarch character: "She, of the limitless dress, the oft-embroidered truth, the rose-scented lies." *Wow, Babs really is a die-hard fan.*

"You all look a*maz*ing!" Ms. Linden said. "Just fan*tas*tic!" She looked at the clock. It was nearly seven. "Okay, everyone, into the supply room like we practiced. Scoot! Scoot! Grace? Wayne!"

Sophie sat on a chair in the supply room, hot under her bulky turtleneck and black sweats, dreading putting on the heavy fencing mask and mittens Ms. Linden had borrowed from the phys ed teacher. She told herself it was just a stupid play that nobody cared about, but she noticed her hands shaking anyway.

So, I'm already sweating buckets, Adnan is chattering and flapping way more than usual, Fiona looks ashen and scared to death, Grace is totally out of it, and Wayne is bellowing down the hallway. Good, good. Plus, we have a demented-looking teacher. All the makings of a flawless production. Thank God I'm wearing this mask for the entire thing.

Alison Hughes

"All right, guys, let's all just take a deep breath. This is going to be just fine." Lucy took her seat in the storage room with a big sigh. She was wearing all black to blend into the shadows while helping, prompting, stagehanding. "And tomorrow I'm bringing in the biggest box of donuts I can buy, and we're watching funny movies all day." She patted Adnan's hand and pulled Grace down into the chair beside her. Wayne cannoned into the room.

"Here, Wayne, here's a seat," Sophie said.

"Right beside Abom'nation." Wayne grinned. "My dear little child."

"You got it," Sophie said. That wasn't in the script, and somehow it made tears come to her eyes to think that Wayne's God character would call Abomination his little child. She blinked them away, looking down and fiddling with the clasps of her mask.

"So, remember, everybody," Lucy said, "there will be those two tenth graders helping me with the lights and stuff. Hassan and Kyle. Really nice guys, you don't have to worry about them. Just listen to Ms. Linden's cues and do the scenes just like we practiced. I'll be right there to help with anything. No pressure."

Noise increased in the classroom outside the supply room door. The sounds of people scraping back chairs, talking, laughing. The audience was in. Soon, they heard Ms. Linden say, "Hassan? I think we can begin." The lights in the classroom went out, and the group in the supply room froze. Fiona grabbed Sophie's mittened hand.

"Relax, Fi. Atmosphere, right?" Sophie whispered.

A high-pitched, metallic screech from the mic as it was turned on, and then Ms. Linden's voice.

"Whoops, sorry. Apologies to all the ears out there, *haha*. Why do mics always do that? Anyway, welcome, welcome, family, relatives, friends, to the Opportunity Class's production of Mariam Gayle's *Abomination*. On behalf of the students and staff, just let me say that we are honored to perform this magnificent play, celebrating difference and differing abilities ..."

Sophie stared at the floor, willing her to stop gushing. She gave the projector cart a little tug. Good. Somebody, probably Lucy, had oiled the wheels. It had been a little sticky in practice.

"Almost time for Mother, Father, Abomination, and Shadowy Friend to do the opening scene," said Lucy. "Wayne, you have to stay here and look after this room for us. Can you do that? You're on *next* scene."

"Yeah, yeah, Lucy, I know, *I* know."

"Grace," Sophie said, "*Grace*! C'mon. Hold my hand. Just stay with me."

"And as it had been, had always been, would always be," Ms. Linden was narrating loudly and theatrically, "a baby born. A little world, a soft island, a shining *sea*."

"Birth scene. Let's go," said Lucy. They walked out into the darkened classroom. The audience was in shadow, and only the "stage" was illuminated by two spotlights.

Lucy threw down the blanket and Fiona slid down on it, Adnan kneeling beside her.

"Remember, hold out your robe, Grace. I'm supposed to hide behind it," Sophie whispered. Getting no reaction, she repeated, "*Arms*, Grace!" Grace spread her arms and walked into the light, Sophie crouch-walking behind her.

"'This monster is no part of me, nor you, nor any mortal soul. It shall not live to see the light of day,' Father screamed." Ms. Linden was really throwing herself into the narration.

Adnan did an awkward karate chop, deflected by Fiona.

"'All innocence is this child!' Mother cried. 'Shadowy Friend, friend of the shadows, take it and cover it and guard it like the secrets of the world.'"

Grace dropped her arms, Sophie leapt into the spotlight, staggered back from Adnan who was karate-chopping randomly now, turned to the audience, and fled with Grace.

Back in the storage closet, they listened while Wayne stole the show. Though sworn to silence, 'God' continued to bellow some of his lines.

"A natural performer, that guy," laughed Lucy, shaking her head.

"That wasn't so bad, hey? Hey? I've only got two, no three more scenes," said Fiona. "You?"

"Three. Almost done." Sophie would never have admitted it to anyone, but it was kind of exciting to be out there in the spotlight. Hearing the audience gasp or murmur or still into silence. There was even a shared excitement among the class in the supply closet, a sense of pulling together.

Maybe Babs was actually right about putting on a play, having something we could all work toward. Maybe I haven't given her enough credit.

The play unfolded. Ms. Linden emoted and shrieked herself hoarse providing the dialogue for everyone. The play built to the final scene — Abomination taking flight. Sophie pushed the cart out of the storage closet with Lucy and Fiona, then climbed on, belly down, legs and arms straight.

"And Abomination saw that her *chains* were broken, her *shackles* worn." Ms. Linden's voice was quivering with emotion. "She was *free*, as free as any creature, now or before. She rose, faceless face raised to the stars, to the limitless skies."

"I think we'll end it there," Ms. Linden had said during rehearsals. "What do you think? A suggestion of limitless possibilities."

"Yeah, why drag everybody down with the real ending," Sophie had said with a bitter laugh, "with old Abbie stumbling toward death?"

Fiona, surprisingly strong in a wiry way, gave the cart a big push, and Sophie glided across the floor into the light, her masked face raised to the spotlights while Lucy and the grade ten boys rippled blue bedsheets to cover the cart. Under the fencing mask, Sophie saw a dazzling pattern of light and darkness, she felt the gust of wind from the sheets and, just for a moment, she felt Abomination's exhilaration as she swooped through the skies, freed from the judgment of other people.

Sophie slid out of the stage light. There was a pause, the audience seemed to want to make sure it was actually over, then they burst into enthusiastic applause. The classroom lights were switched on.

"Thank you, thank you," Ms. Linden was saying. "Our performance of *Abomination* by Mariam Gayle, everyone! Meet our wonderful actors: Wayne, Grace, Fiona, Adnan, and Sophie. With help from our marvelous aide, Lucy Thompson, and our super-special tech assistants, Kyle and Hassan."

Ms. Linden looked terribly white and drained under the fluorescent lights. She was smiling her death's head grin, baring all her teeth. The fake roses in her hair were threatening to fall out, and her shawl trailed on the floor.

Poor Babs, thought Sophie. *I know nothing about her life. Maybe this was the biggest thing in her world, this play, tonight. And now that it's over, she's exhausted. Mental note: tell her she did a great job tomorrow.*

The applause continued for all the kids, spiking when Sophie pulled off her mask and took a bow. As she swept her sweaty hair from her face, she looked into the audience. There were more people there than she had thought. She saw Fiona's mother and little brother, Adnan's parents and grandparents, Wayne's entire loud, extended family.

Wait.

There. At the back of the room. That couldn't be …

It was.

Sitting in the very back row, all by themselves, were her mother and father. A small woman with long black hair rose suddenly from the seat beside her mother, turned sharply, and left the room. Sophie had a fleeting glimpse of the hawkish profile.

Mariam. Sophie's face flushed; her hands went cold.

How on earth …

Ms. Linden grabbed Sophie's arm in an iron grip.

"Sophie," she whispered urgently, "was that her? Was that Mariam Gayle?" She didn't wait for an answer, but bolted for the door, shouldering past people, stumbling over her long shawl.

Sophie stalked into the storage room and stripped off her mask and mitts. Her cold hands were shaking. The thought of her parents and Mariam being there all along made her squirm with embarrassment.

"Done." Fiona smiled. "All done. What a relief."

"Yeah, glad that's over, Fi." Sophie forced a smile for her. "You did great."

"You need a ride home?"

"No thanks. I really, really need some air. Hot in here. See you tomorrow."

Sophie ran down the hallway to the back of the school, clumsily rounding the corner at the end but not actually falling. She let herself out through the gym doors and stood against the wall, the cold air drying the sweat on her face, gulping in deep breaths.

The night was clear, the stars were out.

She was free, for the moment.

She walked the long way home.

Chapter Twelve

BY THE TIME SOPHIE GOT home she was in a white-hot rage.

How dare Babs contact my parents? She clearly didn't trust me to deliver her stupid invitations. Okay, so she was right not to trust me because I burnt them, but still. And Mom, sitting there at dinner, asking me what I was doing tonight, pretending to believe my lies. And Dad, not telling me either. And Mariam. Just being there, just being Mariam.

Sophie stopped in the middle of the sidewalk imagining what Mariam would have thought of that play. Imagining Ms. Linden catching up to Mariam, imagining Ms. Linden's hero worship, imagining Mariam despising her.

Sophie pushed open the front door. As soon as she did, the conversation in the drawing room stopped.

Her instinct said: *kick off your shoes and make a run for the stairs.* She didn't listen to it. She walked straight in. Her mother and father were sitting on opposite ends of the couch, tense and strained. They looked up apprehensively as she came in. Mariam was in a chair, her head on her hand, her legs curled up under her. She didn't look up.

"Congratulations, quite a show," her father began in a hearty voice.

"What the *fuck* were all of you doing there tonight?" she demanded.

"Sophie —"

"Because nobody *fucking* invited any of you. You should never have come."

"Oh, look, Sophronia is so grown up that she can use bad words," Mariam drawled from her chair. "We are all shocked. Appalled."

"Sophie," her mother said quickly, "it was a class play. The other parents were there. You should have told us. As it was, we found out from Ms. Linden, who positively badgered us —"

"This isn't about Ms. Linden!" Sophie roared. "She should never have contacted you. She should have let *me* decide who *I* wanted to come. And it wouldn't have been any of you."

"If we could just talk like civilized people, please," her father said wearily.

"And I'm sure you've all been sitting here bitchily dissecting the way we butchered that precious play. Having a good laugh? How does it feel to slag a bunch of misfits, who, by the way, are worth a *hundred* of you and your so-called friends."

"Sophie, we're not, we weren't —"

"That teacher of yours is a moron," murmured Mariam, sipping her Scotch and shaking her head. "That is a fact. Quite, quite pathetic."

Sophie rounded on her.

"She's actually *kind*. Understand that word? And news flash, *Mari*am!" she spat. "She loves your book, and *your book doesn't deserve it*. It's a shit story. Sooo shitty. Oh, sorry, that's vulgar phraseology. It's an abomination, actually. Trite, overblown, obvious, tedious, pseudo-profound." Sophie was spitting out the adjectives as they came to her.

Silence.

"I know," said Mariam. She raised her dead gray eyes and looked at Sophie. "All true."

Sophie sat down in the nearest chair.

"I've hated that story since it was first published. I hated it while I was writing it. It's been an albatross around my neck."

"We don't need to get into all that now," said Sophie's mother, eyes flashing a warning.

"Maybe we do," said Sophie. "I'm interested. Why did you write it?"

Mariam's thin hand lifted and fell. Her head fell back against the chair.

"Disability was an interest, an obsession, at the time."

"Mariam, don't," said Sophie's father, looking down at his hands.

"Listen to you both," snapped Mariam at Sophie's parents, "'No! Don't! Stop!' Sophronia there is the only one who seems ready to hear the truth. Finally showing a bit of Gayle spirit, for once in her life, and you want to crush it out of her."

"I have none of your Gayle spirit in me, thank God," said Sophie. "I'm Sophie St. John."

Surprisingly, Mariam barked out a harsh laugh.

"Good luck with that, kiddo. The St. Johns will give you more than you bargained for. Well, you want the truth? About *Abomination*?"

"No," Sophie's mother said loudly and got up with a decisiveness that startled them all. "*No*. Not now. Sophie's tired. It's late. That's for a time when we're ready. When we're all ready."

"Ready for what?" asked Sophie. "What do you have to do with her writing *Abomination*? What the hell's going on?"

"Two ostriches," said Mariam cryptically. "Two ostriches with their heads in the sand, that's what's going on." She shrugged. "You always were a coward, Elisabeth. I don't care what you do. I'm tired. Take me back to the hotel, Michael."

Sophie's father got to his feet, feeling his pockets for his car keys. He looked pale. More than pale: old and shaky. He met Sophie's eyes and gave her a forced smile, patting her shoulder as he headed to the door.

As she passed Sophie, Mariam stopped.

"Have you ever looked at when that story was written? No?"

"*Mariam!*" her mother wailed. It was practically a scream.

Mariam shrugged, and with a shake of her dark head, left the room.

Sophie looked over at her mother. She was collapsed in her chair, bent over, her head in her hands.

"Mom?"

Her mother held one bony hand out, straight-armed it like a cop stopping traffic.

Stop, the hand said. No more.

Leave.

Sophie left.

AFTER A HOT SHOWER, SOPHIE lay on her bed, digging into the private stash of junk food she bought with babysitting money. She chewed, angrily, rhythmically, looking at her dark window, shoving chip after chip into her mouth.

She flipped open her laptop and googled "Mariam Gayle Abomination."

A Wikipedia page popped up, and she scrolled down, past sentences like: "A seminal work ushering in a bizarre, stylized form of literary grotesquerie." She'd heard all that before.

Original publication date, that's what she was looking for. There: 2004. Reprinted loads of times, but originally published in 2004.

Which tells me exactly nothing. What was so special about 2004? What did Mariam say as she left? "Haven't you ever looked at when that story was written?" When the story was written. Why? Why would it matter when it was written?

She scrolled down through Plot, a long list of Awards, past Reviews and Appearances to Commentary. Subheading: Inspiration. There was a quote from a *New York Times* book reviewer:

Despite numerous journalistic and academic attempts, famously reclusive Mariam Gayle has consistently refused to illuminate her inspiration for her most influential story, *Abomination*. A radical departure from her other works, the "grotesquerealism" of *Abomination* remains unexplained.

"Gayle prefers to operate opaquely, obliquely," says Dr. Anais Hepworth, Modern English Professor at Eastern University's English Department. "*Abomination* has always remained shrouded in mystery."

So, Mariam never said what prompted her to write the story.

Sophie thought for a moment, then googled "world events 2003-2004." Mariam had always at least pretended to be an activist, lending her name and reputation to a number of causes and then dropping them. Maybe there had been some event at the time that had galvanized her writing. Sophie tapped and clicked. Space shuttle *Columbia* crashed. The Iraq War. Outbreak of SARS, a respiratory illness. Illness, but not a disability. Possibility? Maybe.

George W. Bush elected for a second term. Ronald Reagan died. A tsunami. Other catastrophes. Facebook launched. Facebook. Mariam loathed social media, every form of it. She didn't even have a cell phone. Could *Abomination* somehow be an allegory of the social media platform?

This is so stupid, Sophie thought, slamming her laptop shut. *Mariam's probably just messing with me. Baiting me, like she always has. Pretending to be all mysterious and profound may work for the rest of the world, Mariam, but not for me. I know you. And you're a mean, overrated, pathetic old woman.*

But she remembered the fear in her parents' eyes when Mariam started talking about *Abomination.* They were wary, desperate to head her off. Afraid. Yes, afraid. Why?

They know something. Mariam knows something. Something they don't want me to know.

Her phone vibrated. Text. Text. Text. Theo.

I hate my life
I hate my family
want to run away?

Sophie laughed, the tension draining out of her.

absolutely
don't go without me
where?

Alison Hughes

anywhere
Belgium? Senegal? Vietnam?
Minnesota? I'm Minnesota level here

                                        not Minnesota

cheap. And I'm broke

                                                cold

true
don't care, anywhere
you finished abominating?

                                        done
                                  long story

congrats
that shit is OVER, Ronny!!

But it wasn't over.
That shit was only beginning.

Chapter Thirteen

"WELL, ROOM 107, CONGRATULATIONS ON a huge success last night!" Ms. Linden was trying to be an enthusiastic cheerleader, but she looked seriously ill. She was dead pale and had dark circles under her eyes. The very tip of her nose was pink.

"Getting one of her headaches," Lucy predicted.

Sophie felt a wave of sympathy for Ms. Linden. She remembered Mariam's bored voice saying, *That teacher of yours is a moron. Pathetic.*

Dear lord, what had Mariam said to her? Whatever it was, she doesn't deserve it. She's a good person. At least she tries, at least she cares about other people.

Babs's eyelids were puffy and red, Sophie noticed. Having borne the brunt of Mariam's sharp tongue often and at too early an age, Sophie felt sick to her stomach at the thought of Ms. Linden crying alone at home last night. She had a vivid mental image of her collapsed on her single bed, roses askew, ugly-crying noisily into her pillow.

Stop it, Sophie. She might just have allergies. Or a headache like Lucy said.

When Lucy killed the lights, flicked on the movie, and handed around the box of donuts, Sophie went up to Ms. Linden's desk. Ms. Linden was struggling to open a bottle of pills.

"Here," said Sophie, taking them from her. She expertly twisted and popped the lid. "These things stick."

"Thanks, Sophie. I seem to have a slight headache here that I really need to nip in the bud." She awkwardly gobbled two tablets, biting them back with her lips.

"Hey, Ms. Linden, just wanted to say thanks for all the work you put into the play. It went great, hey? Everyone here's glad it's ov — you know, glad it went well. And I heard lots of compliments about Epiphany Tree." Lie. But a white one.

Ms. Linden brightened. "Did you? Oh, that's so nice to hear. Well, I'm glad … you know, glad you feel it went well."

"So," Sophie said, "I don't know if you actually talked to Mariam —"

Ms. Linden looked away, straightening a pen on her desk.

"I did get a few words with her after the play. I caught her just as she was leaving, as a matter of fact. In hindsight, that was probably a mistake. She must get that sort of thing all the time. It was cold out in the parking lot, she was tired."

"You shouldn't have invited her," said Sophie gently. "That should've been my call."

Ms. Linden nodded.

"I know, you're right. Sorry, Sophie." No challenge. Immediate contrition. It made Sophie like her so much more; in her experience, adults never apologized. "I've just been such a huge fan of hers for so long, and you're such a great kid who's made so much amazing progress in our class that I wanted to show her … I wanted her to *see*." She shook her head helplessly. "A mistake."

"I'm sorry if she upset you or said anything that was, well, rude. She's … Mariam is …"

"The famed artistic temperament? No time for niceties. Probably walking around in a creative haze."

"She's a total bitch," said Sophie bluntly. "She always has been." She'd never said that to anybody other than to her parents and Theo.

Ms. Linden sat back in her chair and looked at Sophie wonderingly.

"I thought I must have caught her at a bad moment. A *really* bad moment."

"There are *only* bad moments with Mariam. Believe me."

"I was totally bewildered by what I considered an unjustified attack on our performance and on me personally. I mean, she doesn't even *know* me. But I can understand why you call her a bitch." Ms. Linden lowered her voice on the word, like she was unused to swearing. They looked at each other and laughed, both freed from the constraints of Mariam's oppressive reputation.

Sophie perched on the corner of Ms. Linden's desk.

"Was she horribly rude to you? Because she can be unbelievably, staggeringly rude. She has been to me. Many, many times."

Ms. Linden's mouth tightened.

"She was." She stopped, then blurted, "She was *vicious*."

"What did she say?"

Ms. Linden frowned as if concentrating.

"Do you know, Sophie, I can't really recall …"

It's embarrassing, right? You're embarrassed. Ashamed. Mariam has that effect. She plants those seeds and watches them grow. Sophronia lumbers like a St. John. Did she say you were a pathetic moron, Babs? Because she said that at home. I'm so sorry. Did you gush, point out your costume expecting grateful, gracious praise and did she ridicule you for it? Never let her in, Babs. Never.

"I think that story — *Abomination* — brings out the worst in her," Sophie said.

Ms. Linden nodded vigorously, not willing to give up her idol completely.

"It's an emotional tale. Loaded, as they say. *Fraught*."

"Did she mention anything about the play? Anything at all?"

"She said some rather uncomplimentary things about the production. Insensitive things. She seemed not to grasp the value of the Opportunity Class. Where we accept everyone on their own terms."

"She call us half-wits or fuck-ups or something?"

"Ahaha. Sophie."

"I'm sure she did. You're just too polite to repeat the insults. Anything else?"

"She did say one curious thing." Ms. Linden leaned in. "After disparaging the production in no uncertain terms, she said, 'but the casting was curiously apt.' Such bitterness! I'll never forget the look on her face. I have no idea what she meant, other than to underline her clear ... discomfort with Wayne in the God-role. She is, I believe, an atheist."

"I think Mariam's uncomfortable with God because he's *just* a notch above Mariam, and she can't stand that," Sophie said. "Look, she was probably messing with you. Just forget it. I've replayed so much shit from Mariam over the years and let it hurt me time and time again, and I don't want you doing that, okay?"

"Okay, I won't." Ms. Linden smiled, then cocked her head to the side. "I'm sorry you've had to deal with so much. You are a wise soul, Sophie, do you know that?"

Sophie held up her hand and Ms. Linden met it with a high five.

Chapter Fourteen

OVER THE SCHOOL YEAR SOPHIE had gone through, as she mentally called them, the "Three Stages of Legal Studies": angry resentment, sullen detachment, and flickering interest.

"You might think about law school someday," her father had said when he'd made her take the option. "It might be a career path. In any event, it's certainly far more useful and relevant than Film Studies or Food Science." The two options she'd checked off. The options she could have taken with Fiona.

But Legal Studies turned out to be one of Sophie's least-loathed courses. Most of the class had entirely checked out and concentrated on playing games on their laptops, so there was zero pressure, socially. The assignments were easy. And she'd warmed to her soft-spoken, diligent teacher, especially after her father had denigrated her lack of legal qualifications.

"She's teaching *Legal Studies*," her father said, "and she barely knows the difference between plaintiff and, and ..." He stared at the wall, his mouth slightly open.

"Defendant?" said Sophie. "Were you struggling to remember *defendant*? Basic legal term, Dad. Law 101."

"Defendant." Her father stood still, looking confused.

"You okay?" Sophie said.

"Respondent and appellant," he murmured to himself, rubbing his forehead. "I bet your teacher pronounces that one a*pple-ant*," he said, frowning as he flipped through her class notes sitting on the dining room table.

Sophie snatched them away before he could criticize her illegible handwriting. It had always been bad, but lately it had been getting so much worse. Really terrible. She often couldn't decipher anything she'd written, even right after class. But she hadn't wanted to bring in her laptop. Her hands were so clumsy, pounding on the keyboard, that she thought she might attract more attention than the zero attention she attracted writing illegibly and privately in a notebook.

"She's actually *nice*, Dad. And no, she's not going to have a law degree when she's only teaching a high school legal studies class. If you're so concerned about qualifications, why don't *you* teach it?"

She pictured her father in his expensive suit at the front of a class, helplessly trying to engage a classroom of totally bored and unresponsive high school students. Strangely, the image cheered her up. Her father and his whole smug law firm were at least as bad as the pedants at her mother's English department. Maybe worse, because their world didn't revolve around literature, but around money. Sharp, St. John LLP specialized in foreclosures.

How many people'd you make homeless today, Dad? She'd ask him something like that when he was annoying her, or when she was in "one of her moods," as her parents said.

Her father either ignored her, didn't hear her, or let her comment drop, fiddling with a fountain pen he'd taken out of his pocket.

"Here," he said, handing it to her, "for taking notes. I find writing flows much easier with this. Less effort. It helps."

"Uh, thanks, Dad," she said, looking down at the gleaming tortoiseshell pen. She was obscurely moved by the gesture. "It's a nice pen. Beautiful. But don't you need it?"

"Oh, I'll get another one." He hovered, seeming strangely unwilling to leave.

Since the weirdness with Mariam, her father and mother had been treating her like a bomb that needed diffusing. Not snapping back at her like they used to, deliberately not reacting. In fact, all of them were hardly ever in the same room together anymore. There was an oppressive, uneasy feeling in the house, a weight of things unspoken, things avoided.

Never ones to have heart-to-heart talks, her parents seemed to be evading all but the most surface of interactions. A "casserole in the oven" Post-it Note here, a "could you throw in a load of laundry?" there. She'd found it impossible to bring up Mariam's cryptic comments after the play, or Mariam's treatment of Ms. Linden. They wouldn't talk about the former and they wouldn't care about the latter.

And here was her father, weeks after the play, lingering in the same room as her. And she just wanted him to leave.

"I need to borrow your laptop so I can use Quicklaw," Sophie said. "We're supposed to research some cases. That okay?"

"Of course, of course." He turned with what seemed like relief, put the laptop on a place mat, and pushed it across the dining room table toward her. She noticed he had taped a bunch of user-names and passwords right under the keyboard.

"Uh, Dad, probably not a great idea to have these right on the keyboard like that. In case it gets stolen or something. Somebody could just get into all your files."

He wasn't listening. He was flipping through her *Studies in Canadian Law* text, shaking his head.

"Almost nothing on causation. A page and a half on remedies! Some of this isn't accurate *at all*. The law is evolving, a 'living tree,' if you will …"

Sophie closed her eyes. *Oh my God, spare me the pedantic lecture, Dad.* But he was off and running, his hands jiggling the change in his pockets, his face relaxed.

"Unlike code-based systems of law, the common law … the common law …" He stopped mid-sentence.

"The common law … what?" she said. He'd been doing this a lot lately. Stopping. Losing his train of thought. Staring off into space.

"Nothing," he snapped. "I've lost the thread. It's … forget it." He swiped a hand over his forehead, looking rattled. He turned away sharply and barked his shin hard on an end table.

"*God damn it!*" he bellowed, slamming the table against the wall. She sat still as he rubbed his leg and then hobbled out of the room. "Off to collect your mother," he called a few minutes later.

Relieved to be alone in the house, Sophie clicked on the Quick-law icon and entered the password. Then, she randomly picked three of the boring search terms the teacher had assigned on the homework sheet. "Negligence," "Foreclosure," and "Defamation." Typing was easier for her than writing, but it wasn't effortless. Stiff fingers, clumsy hands. Lots of double-checking and back-spacing. She finally got the required one-paragraph definition, and found one related Court of Appeal and Supreme Court case for each term. And her homework was done.

She went to log out from the database, then paused.

Defamation. Sort of like slander. The saying or writing of mean or vicious (but possibly true) things about a person in public. According to the case she'd just skimmed, you had to have said the mean things with a view to "lowering the estimation of the person in the eyes of their peers." She'd remembered the legal term; maybe that's why she'd picked it. She remembered looking it up in the dictionary years ago when Mariam had been sued.

Sophie had been about ten and remembered her mother and father tense in the kitchen, arguing, worried, Dad dispensing legal advice to Mariam over the phone. She'd been sued for a lot of money by a writer she'd slagged off publicly in a *New Yorker* interview. Sophie remembered her mother saying tensely, "Mariam's in hot water again." She remembered her father offering to fly out to be on the legal team, and being hurt when Mariam declined the offer, probably rudely.

Sophie wondered whether that defamation case was in the database. She'd never heard what happened. Did a court actually order Mariam to pay up for saying rude and cutting things about somebody? *That would be very, very sweet*, Sophie thought, *because Mariam says rude, cutting things just about every time she opens her mouth, with no penalty ever.*

In the Quicklaw case name search box, she typed *Gayle*. A long list of cases popped up. *Gayle v. Others, Others v. Gayle, R. v. Gayle.* Scrolling down the list, Sophie realized that the defamation case had only been the tip of Mariam's legal iceberg, which went as far back as the 1970s. Sophie found the defamation case. It was a big one ($250,000 awarded in damages against her) because she'd publicly, unrepentantly, and, the court found, untruthfully called another author a child abuser. *Nice, Mariam, nice.* A couple of years later, a charity — a *charity* — sued her for failing to show up for speaking engagements they'd paid her for. *Looks like she took the money and ran*, thought Sophie.

Sophie scrolled down. An international writer's program sued Mariam for a long list of unpaid bills from an extended stay at a five-star hotel. She was sued for pulling out of a speaking tour at the last minute. She was convicted of impaired driving. One of her husbands sued her for spousal support after they split up. A nuisance case. Tax evasion.

Not to be outdone, Mariam had sued a lot as well. She'd sued publishers, agents, accountants, newspapers, magazines, and organizers of literary festivals. She'd sued two husbands for support after divorce. She sued the adult children of dead husband number two in a wills dispute. Sophie nodded grimly as she scrolled down the long list of cases. All of it was so typical of Mariam. Slash and burn, slash and burn.

If all this should, say, be leaked to a news site, would that be defamation? Sophie wondered.

Wait. What was that one? That last one. She scrolled up. There. Nestled among all of Mariam's carnage was the name *Gayle-St. John*.

Mom?

Dad?

Sophie leaned in and clicked on the case. Loading.

Holy hell, had Mom sued her own mother? Sophie settled in to enjoy this. Then she thought: *or had Mariam actually sued her only daughter?* That was the more likely scenario. *It says something about our profound dysfunction as a family that I wouldn't be surprised either way.*

The case came up: *Gayle-St. John v. Lavoie.*

Lavoie. Who the hell is Lavoie? It wasn't one of Mariam's exes. Sophie at least remembered their names, though not often in order.

She skimmed through the summary at the top of the case report:

Wrongful Birth — Negligence — Medical malpractice — Causation — Duty of care — Doctor failing to perceive risk and offer genetic testing of fetus — Child born with genetic disability — Father adopted, unknowing carrier — Mother suing doctor for loss of opportunity to abort and for costs associated with burden of raising disabled child — Failure of doctors to advise of risk of disability.

She frowned. Mariam suing somebody? About a birth? It must be Mariam suing. Mariam's only child, Sophie's mother, Elisabeth, must be the fetus in question. Sophie leaned in on her elbows and reread the headnote and summary again, slowly. Then she scrolled down and read the first few paragraphs, which outlined the facts of the case.

She skittered to a stop, then sat back, staring at the wall above the computer. There was an expensive oil painting there on the dining room wall. It was a rough sketch of a bald human head, but the eyes and mouth had been obliterated, scraped out, over and over by the artist right down to the canvas. It was called *The Modern World*, and she'd hated it ever since she was a child. What kind of parents would hang such a disturbing thing where a child could stare in horror at it? She didn't even see the painting now. It had no focus, she looked past it, through it.

Because the case she was looking at had nothing to do with Mariam.

It's Mom.

Mom brought this case to court.

This was an appeal. She checked when the case came to trial. 2002. The year she was born.

Sophie went completely cold. Cold in her hands, cold in her feet, cold all the way through.

The case is about me.

My case.

I'm the wrongful birth.

Chapter Fifteen

SOPHIE FELT THE WHOLE WORLD hush. Utter silence, within her and outside of her. It was as if even the house held its musty old breath. She felt suspended, poised, at a danger point between the unknown and the known.

I can stop reading. I can stop right here, right now. I don't have to read this. I can run for the exit, click that little x in the box, and slam the computer shut.

But she knew too much already. And what she knew, no closed computer could hold.

Haven't you always wanted the truth? The voice inside her was insistent. *Haven't you always known it was there, somewhere? Something that explained all the weirdness?*

Maybe not. Maybe I don't. Maybe I never understood that the truth might not be simple. Maybe the truth is a terrible, terrible thing. Maybe ignorance and delusion are way, way safer.

Stop. She took a deep breath, eyes flicking back to the laptop.

She straightened her spine, which had caved gradually as she sat thinking.

Heart pounding so hard that she heard the blood whooshing in her ears, mouth dry, Sophie started reading.

Gayle-St. John v. Lavoie

(2002) Court of Appeal (Eastern District)

Roy, Brezinski, and Cutcheon JA

Per Cutcheon JA, for the court:

1. Facts

The facts of this tragic case are as follows. At thirty-six years of age, Elisabeth Gayle-St. John [hereafter "the appellant"] discovered she was pregnant. The pregnancy was neither planned nor desired by either herself or her husband, Michael Gayle-St. John.

The appellant testified that the couple had hitherto decided against having a child for a number of reasons. Both parties were building successful careers, the appellant establishing herself as an academic, her husband attaining a partnership at a law firm. Further, the appellant battles with depression and anxiety and had serious concerns about how pregnancy and child-rearing could affect her mental health. Finally, owing to her husband's adoption as an infant, there was no information about his genetic medical history.

Notwithstanding the above, when the pregnancy was confirmed, the appellant came to terms with the disruption to her career and her life, and the couple decided to continue with the pregnancy.

How incredibly brave of you, Mom. Having a baby like everyone else in the world, like women have done for the whole of human history. Denying the world, what? A few months of scholarship on Dickens for the slight matter of bringing a child, a life, into the

world. Mrs. Silva had five children — five! — and I've never heard
about her suing anybody for having them.

Ms. Gayle-St. John sought the assistance of her long-term family physician, Dr. Lavoie, for her prenatal care and delivery. She placed considerable trust in him, despite his being an elderly physician past retirement age. The appellant testified that Dr. Lavoie told her he "was experienced" in prenatal care and "kept up" with all the latest developments. Dr. Lavoie, it is worth noting, was not the appellant's husband's physician, and indeed never met him.

The crux of this case came at an appointment with Dr. Lavoie on April 21st, 2002, during the appellant's first trimester. The appellant states that at this appointment she indicated that while her husband currently enjoyed good health, his family history was unknown because he was adopted as a baby, in circumstances rendering the identification of his biological parents impossible. She argues now that this conversation should have raised in the doctor an apprehension that genetic testing of her developing fetus should have been performed.

Sophie's phone vibrated. Theo.

need girl advice
you're a girl right?

She muted the phone. *Bad time, Theo.*

Dr. Lavoie presented his medical notes, which show only that, after some questioning, the appellant indicated that her husband enjoyed good health. When pressed, he admitted that he did not, in fact, ask any probing questions of the appellant about her husband's genetic history. Moreover, he did not ask to question the appellant's husband.

Dr. Lavoie characterized the appellant as a "perfectly healthy" though "neurotic" woman, prone to worrying excessively without rational cause. Had he been expected to follow up on each of her concerns, he testified, he would not have had time for any of his other patients.

I can only imagine the total nightmare my pregnant mother would have been to you, Dr. Lavoie. Freaked out, constantly worrying, rushing in to consult you about every single little thing, every twitch and gurgle. I've had a lifetime of her fretting and fussing about my health.

My health.

Read, Sophie. Read.

Dr. Lavoie neither referred the appellant for genetic testing, nor mentioned it to her. She and her husband therefore trusted that Dr. Lavoie thought the pregnancy was progressing normally.

Despite almost weekly visits to the doctor, the appellant had an uneventful pregnancy.

Approaching full term, at thirty-six weeks, the subject of this case, baby Sophronia, was born. While she presented normally, routine postnatal blood testing revealed that she was in fact born with the genetic disability Juvenile Huntington Disease [hereafter JHD].

Sophie sat back in her chair. She stared at the wall above the computer, her breathing shallow and quick.

Oh, dear God, I have some sort of genetic disease. Juvenile Huntington Disease, whatever that is. I had it as a baby. I was born with it. I have it now. It's deep inside of me, inside of my genes. Something serious enough to have a court case about.

Fragments of memories rolled through her mind, like the first pebbles of a landslide. Doctor's appointments. Therapies and therapists. Counsellors. An only child, she'd assumed it was all normal, what most kids go through, or maybe a product of her mother's obsessive, depressive, morbid worrying. "A very difficult adolescence," was how she'd heard her mother describe it on the phone. The ortho guy, the physio, the yoga: *it's for your hands, Sophie, for your clumsy feet, for your stiffness, for your coordination.* The therapists: *it's so you can manage your anger, Sophie, control yourself better.* The testing, the tutoring: *it's to train your mind, Sophie, you just need a bit more help because your marks have been sliding at school.*

And always, always, the feeling that there was something hidden, something in the background. Something she didn't know. It was elusive. Her dropping something and her mother freezing, a sharp look between her parents at another defiantly presented, pathetic report card. Guarded doctor's messages on the voicemail. The shift into the Opportunity Class for more "one-on-one" assistance.

The growing realization that other kids didn't seem to have as many problems as she had.

"You have *another* doctor's appointment?" She remembered always-healthy Theo asking incredulously. "You seem to have one, like, every week! I literally can't remember the last time I went to the doctor. I don't think I even *have* a doctor. I think it must be all in your mom's mind. Or at least, whatever sickness you have, it's got to be on the *inside*, because you look totally normal."

A sickness on the inside …

Sophie wanted to stop reading, wanted to slam the computer shut. She wanted to unsee those terrible, alien, dangerous words: *Juvenile Huntington Disease*. But it was all too late. The words were tunneling themselves into her brain like worms into soft earth.

The truth, her truth, was here in front of her.

She wiped her clammy hands down the sides of her thighs, caught her breath in a long, shaky sigh, and looked back down at the screen.

The diagnosis of the disease was made by Dr. Strickland, a neurologist specializing in Huntington Disease. The appellant called him as an expert medical witness who confirmed that JHD is a disease that could have been identified through testing on the developing fetus *in utero*. At trial, he attested to the gravity and severity of the condition:

> From conception and certainly after the appearance of
> the primitive streak at 15 days gestation, the embryo
> could have shown the disease through diagnostic
> genetic testing.
> Juvenile Huntington Disease is a serious, rare,
> neurodegenerative disease causing increasing and
> progressive loss of control over movement, emotion,

and thought. The prognosis for the disease is
unfortunately not a happy one: there is no cure.

Sophie stared at those words, the last two, the *no cure* words.

All her clumsiness, her outbursts, her memory lapses explained so baldly, so unemotionally in one dry sentence. *Progressive loss of control over movement, emotion, and thought. So: everything,* Sophie thought. *Loss of control over everything — over my whole, entire self, over my brain and my body and my emotions. The loss of me.*

There is no cure. She stalled at that sentence, rereading it over and over.

She didn't feel the tears slipping down her cheeks until they dripped from her chin to her neck.

She didn't know what this "primitive streak" was that this Dr. Strickland was talking about, but the phrase resonated deeply. She felt her own primitive streak well up deep within her, a screaming red mass of raw terror, of pain and death and nonexistence. A wild, panting, cornered animal with only two options: fight or run.

She angrily scrubbed her tears away.

Fight.

Read.

Moreover, Dr. Strickland stated that the average life expectancy for children and young adults afflicted with JHD is fifteen years post-diagnosis or after the onset of symptoms.

Fifteen years?? I can't have only fifteen years left of living. Can I?

She reread the sentence, her hand over her mouth. "Post-diagnosis." *I was apparently diagnosed as a baby, so haha! I've lasted sixteen years already.* She fought back a ghastly, burbling terror-giggle.

"After the onset of symptoms" was her better bet. She could maybe squeeze a few more years out of that one. How long had she had symptoms? What kind of symptoms? Loss of control over movement, emotion, and thought? All of them? Or only one? Only some?

"Sophronia lumbers like a St. John," in ballet when she was eight, according to smoking Mariam. Sophronia falls down the stairs and breaks her arm and collarbone in grade five. Sophronia cries a lot in grade seven, and not only because of the mean girls. Sophronia's marks start tanking. When? Grade nine for sure, but that was when she started secretly drinking and she always blamed it on that. Sophronia throws a chair in grade eleven English class. Sophronia blacks out in Art Therapy.

She could have far fewer than fifteen years left.

Read. Just be brave enough to read it all, she thought.

This is the story, right here. This is the truth.

And you've never been told the truth.

Crucially, for the purposes of this case, JHD is a hereditary disease. Subsequent genetic testing of the appellant's husband, Sophronia's father, revealed that he shares the Huntington Disease gene, albeit not in the Juvenile form.

Dad stumbling and falling when he goes running with the Greyhounds. Dad forgetting the word "defendant." Dad losing his train of thought. Dad banging into furniture. Poor Dad. How long does he have left? Is it the fifteen years for adults, too?

Sophie steadied her head with both her hands. They felt ice cold against her hot face.

So. First section of the case was a doozy. The facts.

On to a new section.

Let's hope it picks up! The dreadful heaving, sobbing giggle welled up again, and Sophie clamped her hand over her mouth.

Chapter Sixteen

AS SOPHIE READ, WHAT AT first seemed complex became crystal clear, simple really: her mother sued her doctor. The action was called "wrongful birth," a really horrid phrase, Sophie thought. It was almost unbelievable, but her mother had claimed, in a court of law, that she was owed money because her doctor hadn't referred her for genetic testing, which would have shown fetus-Sophie's disability and enabled her mother to have an abortion.

And I would never have existed. Hard to wrap my mind around that one.

Her parents had, in the words of the court, "been deprived of an opportunity to exercise their parental choice to terminate the pregnancy." Sophie almost laughed. *Deprived of an opportunity* made it sound like they missed out on a real estate deal. A Black Friday sale. *Don't miss this opportunity to abort! Limited time offer!*

She read on about other cases, other parents who'd been deprived of that opportunity, and about cases of "wrongful life," where people born with disabilities had to argue they should never have been born at all in order to get money to pay for the care they needed to live.

And behind it all, behind the legal and medical jargon, was the sweeping, breathtaking assumption in all the cases that having a disability makes you a hindrance, a burden, a lesser human being. Their births: wrongful. Their lives: wrongful.

Sophie thought of Wayne, rattling off the sports stats, giving everyone huge hugs, making them all laugh. She thought of Adnan, alone in that world of his, following the rules his unique mind decreed. Then Charlie, helplessly barking out obscenities and rage, but otherwise a sweet and kind guy. Just something different deep within him.

They should have been born. Of course, they all should have been born. None of them is "wrongful" in birth or in life. They're as worthy of life as anyone. "Worthy." What a supremely useless word. Worthy of what? Worth what? To whom? Who decides someone else is worthy to exist or not? Them? Their parents? Society? This court?

2. The Trial Court Decision

At trial, the judge rejected the appellant's claim.

Holy shit, Mom lost?

Sophie straightened up, galvanized by this ruling. Yes, her mother (and, let's be honest, her father, lurking in the shadows of this judgment but probably pulling the strings) had lost the case, the trial judge ruling against her. The combination of her mother's harassment of poor old Dr. Lavoie during her pregnancy — described as "an avalanche of endless, almost daily queries, concerns, and worries" — and the rarity of the disease, her disease, led the judge to conclude that it was unreasonable to hold Dr. Lavoie liable for not offering testing.

Consensus seems to be that Mom was a total pain-in-the-ass patient. Dad would have been so furious to lose at trial. "Cattle court," that's what he calls trial court. That's got to have hurt.

Sophie pictured younger versions of her mother and father sitting in their living room, her mother possibly feeding or rocking their inconvenient, defective baby, plotting their appeal about her very wrongful birth, considering angles, rejecting approaches, brainstorming wording.

How could they?

She sucked in a deep, shaky breath. The feeling of betrayal was almost more than she could bear.

Read. We're on to their appeal of my case, just when poor old Dr. Lavoie probably thought he was safe, when he was probably hoping for a peaceful retirement.

But it's also my life they're talking about. I'm dying, literally dying, to hear what happens.

3. The Appeal

Blah, blah, blah. Wow, these judges do not ever get to the point … Here. This is an important part:

Dr. Lavoie failed to offer any testing for any infirmity, disease, or disability. The law does not require physicians to be clairvoyant, predicting the precise condition for which to order testing. It does, however, require physicians to take whatever reasonable steps a similarly situated physician would take. Here, further questioning would have led any reasonably diligent physician to offer genetic testing.

Sounds like Cutcheon J's going with team Gayle-St. John ...

Sophie skipped down to the next section titled "The Abortion Question." Apparently, ludicrously, her mother had to not just claim but *prove* that she would have aborted a disabled fetus, that this wasn't some abstract, whimsical idea she had that she wouldn't really have gone through with.

Helpfully, she provided the court with an itemized list of proofs: the pregnancy was unwanted and unplanned (they were using contraception), her feminist beliefs about the right to abortion, her lack of moral or religious opposition to abortion, her history of anxiety and depression making her an "unsuitable candidate for bearing and rearing a disabled child."

Sophie blinked at the bullet point saying that her mother had had a previous abortion when she was a teenager. *Whoa. Nobody ever told me about that. Mom didn't know Dad until they were in university. I could have had an older sister. An older brother.*

The last bullet point stated that, during her undergraduate degree, Elisabeth accompanied Mariam Gayle, her mother, when Ms. Gayle terminated two pregnancies.

Never heard about those, either. We could have been a big family: aunts, uncles, possible cousins ...

The judge summarized that these factors "cumulatively prove" that her mother definitely, without question, undoubtedly would have had an abortion.

Way to go, Mom. You proved it! And how do I ever, ever deal with all that? It all sounds so logical, so reasonable, until you're the one being aborted. Then it doesn't sound logical or reasonable at all. It all gets way more complicated.

I don't think I can take much more of this, Sophie thought, rubbing her eyes.

She scrolled down. There were only a few pages left. A few more crucial pages titled *Damages*.

The word seemed appropriate on a lot of levels. It was how she was feeling. Damaged, wrecked. Damage to her, damage to her mother, damage to her already damaged relationship with her parents. The damage spiraled out into the future, a whole, shortened life of it.

But here, *Damages* was legalese for compensation, for money.

Damages was the payoff, the jackpot for arguing (and proving) that your baby should never have existed.

Her phone vibrated.

Theo sending a cute baby animal video. Otters.

Chapter Seventeen

4. **Damages**

a. **General Damages**

The appellant argues that she is owed a sum of money in general damages for bearing the burden of parenting a disabled child who, had she been given full information through prenatal genetic testing, they would have aborted.

I find no merit in that submission.

To characterize this baby's entire existence as a form of harm warranting compensation profoundly denigrates her life and the lives of all those who live with disabilities.

SOPHIE COVERED HER FACE WITH her hands as the tears fell. It was unexpected, this small kernel of human kindness in an otherwise cold, clinical case. And it came from a stranger. After a while, she wiped her eyes and nose on her sleeve.

Thank you, dear, dear judge. Judge ... what the hell is your name again? Sophie scrolled up. *Cutcheon J. Thank you, dear, dear Cutcheon J. Thank you for not allowing them to denigrate my life. I had never heard of you until I started reading this case ten minutes ago (which seems like ten years ago), and yet you are suddenly my closest friend. My first baby-self's friend. Taking my side against my own parents, who, if they couldn't have me dead, bloody well wanted somebody else to pay for the burden that is me.*

This court, any court, is ill-equipped to answer phil-osophical questions about the value of a life. Can life, disability, and nonexistence be quantified? Is this baby's life preferable to her never having lived at all? How can we calculate the joy and love a baby, even one subject to a serious disease, brings to a family to offset their pain and suffering? These questions cannot be answered in a court of law. The law of torts, indeed any law at all, pales in comparison to their enormity.

I therefore award no damages on this front.

Sophie stared at the wall, her eyes blurred with tears. *Joy. Love.* Words that sounded like a foreign language in this house, in this family. Had she ever really known either of those things with her parents? Had they known those things with her? Had they kept a tally, checking it occasionally to see if, on balance, she had brought them enough joy and love to offset their pain and suffering at her being born at all?

b.   Damages relating to lost parental choice

The damage to the appellant here is better characterized as lost parental choice and autonomy. Mrs. Gayle-St. John was owed a duty of care by her physician to have all the information about her fetus that was reasonably available at the time. This court must, therefore, find the physician negligent. I will briefly survey similar cases with a view to

Sophie scrolled quickly down past the case excerpts, appalled at the casual cataloguing of other people's despair. She averted her eyes; peeking at even isolated words was like slowing down to gawk at a traffic accident. *Deformity, severe malfunction, coma, perforated, degenerative, vegetative.* So many babies whose parents argued they'd have aborted them had they known what they really were. So much sadness and misery. She stopped scrolling when Cutcheon J. finally summarized.

> After reviewing these cases, which similarly grappled with the problem of lost parental choice in wrongful birth, and considering this case to be on a similar footing in relation to damages, I award damages under this heading in the sum of $300,000.

Wow. $300,000 for not being given a choice. Theo would say, dorkily, "That's a lot of ka-ching!" She could just see him: face alight and eager, big smile ...

Sophie came to the heading **c. Damages for Mental Anguish and Emotional Distress**. The judge outlined the trial judge's findings of the serious nervous breakdown her mother had after she was born.

A nervous breakdown. Her father had once told her that her mother "had a bit of a tough time after you were born." He didn't elaborate. Sophie had assumed he'd meant regular things everyone experiences adjusting to life with a newborn baby. No sleep. Problems breastfeeding. Or irregular things only her parents would find tough: no time to reread Dickens, having a lean publication year, not being able to have regular dinner parties.

But here was Cutcheon J. outlining months of depression and therapy and "suicidal thoughts" never even divulged to her therapist.

Sophie closed her eyes on a wave of guilt and sadness. Her mother — lost in the darkness, suffering, despairing ...

Nick wandered into the room, gave his flat *rrrowww*, and rubbed against her leg. Sophie leaned down and stroked him, grateful for the contact.

Then resentment and rage elbowed guilt out of the way, cleansed her, freed her. She'd been duped before, been lied to, been guilted by her parents so many, many times. Was this, too, a lie?

Suicidal thoughts you didn't tell your therapist about? So, no witnesses. Did you and Dad think the worst possible scenario would get the biggest possible payoff? Was all this to give you a strategic advantage in court?

Nothing, nothing you two did would surprise me now.

Sophie scrolled down.

What did she get for all this terrible mental anguish and emotional distress, Cutcheon J.? In dollars. Ah, here we go:

> Having regard to these precedents, and the depth and severity of the appellant's trauma surrounding this birth, I award damages of $120,000 for her mental anguish and emotional distress.

This is adding up here, even with my math. And we're not done yet! Even more damages in this next section. "Damages for costs of care" for baby Sophronia, for me, for "the rest of her natural life." According to the judge, these costs are so that "the growing child can

*attain her full potential to the extent that is possible." That's a hell of
a depressing qualifier. But look! Even more depressing things!*

Sophie numbly scanned the long list of expenses that her
mother had claimed:

- costs of assistance (assistive devices, ventilators,
  special care aides, health care aides, speech therapists,
  physiotherapists)
- costs of medical needs (nutritional supplements and
  procedures, walkers, wheelchairs, hospital beds)
- aids to daily living (the installation of grab bars,
  commode chair, roll-in shower, special skills dog,
  renovations to home to accommodate wheelchair,
  specialized transport)
- educational assistance (specialized computers and
  programs, special needs camp)
- respite care

These helpfully bulleted and itemized expenses appalled
Sophie like nothing in the judgment had before. In a neat and
orderly way, they presented the utter bleakness of her future life,
one she could never have imagined for herself. Dependent in so
many ways on other people. Dependent, period. A world of walkers and wheelchairs and commode chairs (whatever those are).
People feeding her, helping her have a bath. Strangers in the bathroom with her. Being babysat like she babysits Crystal next door.

*This feels completely unreal. Terrifying. There has to be a mis-
take here somewhere.*

*This has to be a fraud, Mom and Dad fraudulently claiming
my disability to screw this poor doctor (or his insurance company;*

there was something in here about doctors and medical negligence
insurance) out of hundreds of thousands of dollars.

There were only a few more sentences left of the judgment.
Cutcheon J. was wrapping up the whole mess:

> ... taking into account the reduced life expectancy of
> the baby due to her genetic disability, I accept the appel-
> lant's claim of the extent of damages under this heading of
> $550,000.
>
> The total award of damages to the appellant therefore
> totals $970,000.00.

And that was it. Everybody packed up and went home.

There was nothing more to read.

Was justice done? What even *was* justice here?

Sophie slowly lowered her head down to the table. She crouched
there for a long time.

Then her head snapped up. Like the dutiful Legal Studies student she was, she checked whether that case, her case, had been
appealed. Mom and Dad lost at trial, won on appeal. Did poor
old Dr. Lavoie appeal to the Supreme Court?

There it was. Two years later. He did.

Appeal denied.

So ultimately, we completely won, thought Sophie.

Yay us!

The hysterical laughter bubbled up again and she bit the inside
of her lip until she tasted blood.

Blood.

*My blood, my defective blood. The blood my defective father
passed down to me.*

She lurched to her feet, the pen her father had given her falling from her lap and rolling under the piano, the chair she'd been sitting on crashing backwards. At the sound, Nick tore out of the room.

Her heart was skittering, skipping, making her breathless and light-headed. She paced erratically, trying to corral her galloping, disjointed thoughts.

Three main facts. If this is not a fraud, this whole thing comes down to three main facts.

Three massively important, crucial, world-shaking main facts.

First fact: I have a terrible disability.

Second fact: I am at best middle-aged, and at worst old-aged.

Sophie's mind shied away from those two facts, to the only one that seemed to have a possible upside.

Third fact: I am possibly very rich.

Chapter Eighteen

SOPHIE HAD RIGHTED HER CHAIR and was sitting back at the dining room table, feeling exhausted and many years older, when she heard her parents come in. She glanced at the clock. Unbelievable: it had only been an hour since Dad had gone to pick up Mom? An *hour*.

"Still at the homework?" Her father barely looked at her as he walked into the kitchen with two bags of takeout food. Her mother was taking forever unlacing those ridiculous, finicky granny boots she wore. Her querulous voice wafted in from the front entrance.

"... and Addison Phelan's applied for tenure! Michael, did you hear me? *Addison*. Not one publication this *decade* after that dreadful novella, *Venus Shrugged*, you remember that Marxist one ... (Oh. Hi, Sophie. Dinner's Vietnamese. From that place on campus)" — she headed into the kitchen — "and student evaluations that are rock-bottom. I've seen them. Worse than Craven. Worse than *Wachovski*, and that's really saying something."

Sophie heard them pull containers out of the plastic bags, assemble bowls, rummage for the lacquer chopsticks, all to the drone of her mother's voice. Sophie heard the cadence of the litany of complaint and criticism, not really the words. It was always the same. Everyone was stupid except them. Never a light-hearted moment. No attempt at generosity. Nobody'd be bringing them cakes like Mrs. Silva, that's for sure. Their workplaces were war zones where they aimed to be the last people standing.

Sophie felt trapped in floating sense of unreality, a deep, profound weirdness.

Everything felt strange. The very chair she was sitting on felt odd. The table, the house. Sophie looked over at her parents, and they were strangers, too. She was seeing them for the very first time. Her mother, small and bony, tragic maroon pixie cut, scrawny neck poking out of an oversized sweater. Dumping pho into a beautiful ceramic bowl because she couldn't bear to eat out of takeout containers. Fussy, precise little movements, irritable with her father's clumsiness.

"Do you have the spring rolls? Because if they forgot them again …"

Her father, tall and broad, a carefully camouflaged bald spot on the top of his head, expensive casual wear. He did lurch, Sophie realized. He was lurching right now, lunging and swinging to catch one of the cardboard dividers sliding off the end of the counter. How had she never noticed that? His legs were stiff, his hands shaky as he handed her mother the spring roll container.

Watching him, Sophie remembered that the judgment said he had this disease too. Some form of it. A cold fear closed around her heart. How much time did he have left? Did his heartiness cover secret despair? Were his renovations obsession and his determined running ways of avoiding or simply forgetting? How would her mother cope without him?

"I've sacked the flooring fellow," he said. *Sacked,* instead of *fired,* Sophie noted, closing her eyes. *Fellow* instead of *guy. Queue* for *line-up. Git* rather than *jerk.* The "Ye-Olde-English-isms," as

Theo had once called them. Irritating for so long. Now all she felt was sad.

"… tore a strip off him. Brian recommended another fellow, so I rang him up. Should get back to me tomorrow."

They assembled the dinner somebody else had made, neither of them knowing or caring how she was feeling right now, at this moment. Her life, her whole life, was wrongful. She was defective, expendable, resented. They had never wanted her, never known her.

Neither knew that her world had been ripped to shreds.

Neither knew she knew.

Watching them, Sophie felt a rush of dark, hot rage sweep over her. The primitive streak inside of her rearing its ancient, vicious, ravenous head. She welcomed the rage. It burnt away all the betrayal and guilt and sadness and terror into rubble, leaving only glaring white-hot anger. Her rage made her stronger. Righteous.

Her stomach rumbled.

Traitor.

Her mother and father came into the dining room and set the table around her, fussy, tight-lipped, irritated that she wasn't moving or helping. They continued their disjointed conversation about the crucial flooring issue.

"… tried to sell me engineered hardwood. Practically plywood …"

"… if he can start Tuesday next, I can move that discovery of documents …"

Sophie's mother glanced over at her.

"Are you eating with us?"

"Well, I'm here, aren't I?" *Aren't I? Whether you like it or not, I'm here.*

"Well," her mother said, in the careful voice that said she was deliberately not rising to the level of the rudeness offered to her, "you almost always take a plate of food to your room, so ..."

Not trusting herself to speak, Sophie just shoved her father's laptop to the end of the table and reached for a place mat.

"*Careful*, Sophie. That'll scratch the finish!" Her father licked the tip of one finger and scrubbed at imaginary scratches on the tabletop.

There he was, dying of his own debilitating disease, obsessing about flooring and table scratches. Sophie wanted to laugh. Or cry. Mostly cry.

Her mother ladled out three bowls of pho and set them on plates. Sophie closed her hands around her bowl, grateful for the warmth seeping into her cold hands. She tried to sip a spoonful, but it felt as though her throat had closed up. She couldn't swallow. *Breathe.* The spoon rattled as she set it back down on her plate.

"How was school?" her mother asked automatically, looking down at her soup. The book of literary criticism was there at the ready, but she hadn't opened it yet. At her father's right was the business section of the newspaper. This was how her parents ate, each reading. Parallel eating.

Her father glanced up, mopping his chin with a napkin.

"Sophie. Your mother asked you a question."

"Actually," said Sophie. It came out in a feeble croak. She cleared her throat. "Actually, I have a question for both of *you*. Why didn't you ever tell me you sued your doctor after I was born?"

Her father froze, a shaky spoonful of pho almost at his mouth. Her mother put down the spring roll she'd picked up.

"Wrongful birth. I mean, I understand it's not exactly something you'd tell a toddler. Or a child. Unless you're someone like

Mariam. But I'm almost seventeen. Were you going to bury the truth forever?"

"Did someone … did Mariam —" Her mother's voice was strained, unnatural.

"Tell me? Did Mariam tell me? Ah, of course she knows. I didn't know, but she did. No, surprisingly, she didn't. Although I'm sure she's been dying to tell me all these years. How sweet for her to know all along I wasn't wanted —"

"Sophie —"

"— that I was disabled, that you wanted me *dead*," she screamed. This was not quite the cold, dispassionate tone she had aimed for when she began this conversation.

"*Sophronia!*" Her father's voice sounded strangled.

"It's true. It's the truth! Sorry if it hurts. So sorry if it *upsets* you both."

"I don't want —" said her mother shakily.

"I don't *care* what you want or don't want! *I* want to talk about this. I do. *Me.* I want to hear the truth, not from some judge on Quicklaw, but from *you*."

"Did you read the case?" her father said quietly. "Did you actually read all of it?"

"No, *Dad*," she said, dripping sarcasm. "I saw it was about you guys wanting me dead, and me having a terrible disability and all, and so I thought: you know what? Maybe I better just let dear old Mom and Dad tell me this one. Whenever they want to get around to it."

"Don't," said her mother. But Sophie raised her voice and talked over her.

"Oh, right — you never did! You never did tell me this one. *Of course*, I read the case, Dad. And what a really terrific, really stellar way of me hearing about how much you loved me as a baby. And my long and happy future! Really, you guys should have your own section in the parenting books." She dashed away the tears that were running down her face.

"Listen to me," her father said urgently. "Wrongful birth —"

"My God." Sophie stared at him. "You're going to give me a lecture about fucking *tort law*, aren't you?" Her head dropped to her hands. "I can't believe this."

"— was the only way! That doctor *was* negligent, Sophie! Wrongful birth was our only option for damages. Don't you see? To punish his negligence, yes, but also to have a fund for your eventual … care."

"Ah, right. For me. You wanted me dead, but if not, you wanted me to have lots of money. That makes total sense, Dad. It couldn't possibly be because you were furious at Dr. Lavoie?"

"He was negligent. That was clear. He didn't refer us —"

"— for the genetic testing. Yeah, I *read* the thing, Dad."

"Well, in a wrongful birth action, the parent, parents, are constrained. They have to argue certain things." He glanced at his wife, who had her eyes closed, one hand propping up her head.

"You're telling me you *had* to say you'd have aborted me?"

"That's the essence of the claim! Lack of parental agency. That had we had the requisite information —"

"Fuck's sake, Dad, I *get* it, okay? Do you honestly think it's going to make me feel better hearing you *say* you'd have aborted me?"

"I don't honestly know what we'd have done," Sophie's mother said quietly, "even had we known the whole truth."

This shut everyone up for a second.

"That's easy to say now, when you're cornered, Mom. When you have a real, live sixteen-year-old in front of you. It's not what you said then. It's not what you said in court," she shouted. "You swore to a judge you'd have aborted me. You brought in proof! This one's defective. *Pffft!*" Sophie made a thumb-over-the-shoulder gesture. "Outta there. Like the one before, when you were a teenager! Like Mariam's two — the both of you killing babies right, left, and center. You ever think about *them*, Mom?"

"Of course, I do," her mother snapped, energized by anger. "You have no idea, none at all. Listen to yourself. 'Killing babies'? God, you sound like some fundamentalist bible-thumper. It was our right! We have the *right* to control our own bodies." She was breathing hard, erratically. In a deadly little voice, she asked, "Are you seriously questioning a woman's right to have an abortion?"

"No, Mom. Do not do that. Do not turn this into an academic debate on abortion. This is not abortion in the abstract. Abortion as an idea, as birth control. This is *me*. This is about my life. This is about you fighting in court for the right to abort *me!*" Sophie despised herself for breaking down on that final, strangled word.

"We're losing sight of the point of the case," said her father desperately. "The point of the case was not only to prove Dr. Lavoie liable for negligence. It was also to ensure there was enough money to care for you for the rest of your life."

"Which, I hear from old judge blah-blah there, isn't actually going to be much of a life, hey Dad? Not a normal life. Or a very long one. Yeah, that's something else I read on Quicklaw. I've got a terrible disability that nobody told me about before. Nice of that *judge* to let me know."

"Sophie, believe me, we never wanted you to find out like this," her mother said. She reached out her hand awkwardly across the table, but Sophie flinched away.

"Don't touch me!"

"Listen, then. We wanted to take it step by step, see how you were doing, wait for the right time. And you've been doing well! *Really* well. Everyone said so. The life of a normal child." Her mother's eyes behind her thick glasses were huge, welling with tears.

"Really, Mom? What do you know about normal children? I'm in the Opportunity Class. I black out sometimes. I feel such *rage*. My hands are clumsy, and my legs are stiff, and I lumber, and I go to doctors and therapists, and I threw a chair at Mr. Green and oh, my God, I'm losing control of thought and emotion and ... one more thing. 'Progressive loss of control over *blank* and emotion and thought.' Movement! That's it. Movement as well. So, I'm right on track with this disease or disability or whatever, folks."

Her mother stood up abruptly, swayed a little.

"We'll go see the Huntington Disease specialist now you're having ... experiencing ... You've seen him before, but you were young. You can talk to him privately if you want." She hesitated, putting a shaking hand to her temple. "I can't cope with all this right now. My head is splitting ..."

"Poor Mom. Sorry. Hard for you." Sophie hated how mean and hard she sounded. But that's how she was feeling. A raw, red thing with sharp, snapping teeth and a voice hoarse from screaming, a primitive thing.

"I'll talk to her, Elisabeth," her father said. "We'll work this out." Her mother nodded without looking at him and stumbled from the room. Sophie heard dragging footsteps going up the stairs.

Her father turned to her.

"The whole court case was very hard on your mother," he said. "She was very … upset at the time, and she went through some very dark times. *Very* dark times." His mouth twisted, and he looked down.

Had she actually been suicidal? Was that true?

Sophie sat in silence, arms crossed, wavering.

"Did you force her to do it? Were you the one behind the case?"

"You make that sound like it was something terrible!" Her father looked genuinely bewildered. "That doctor was negligent. He was liable. That was justice!"

"And what about me, Dad? Where's my justice? What do you say to me?"

"What I say," he said almost eagerly, "is that the case resulted in a very high award of damages. In fact, it set the standard for successive 'wrongful birth' cases!"

The money. He's talking about the money, she realized, all the rage draining out of her, leaving her a cold, empty, desiccated shell. She shook her head.

"Excellent, Dad. Congrats on your legal triumph. Hope Mom made the textbooks."

"Sophie, be reasonable! Think logically. You would have been born with that disease anyway —"

"Not if somebody killed me first!"

He grimaced irritably at her interjection. *Truth is a bitch*, she thought.

"— so, best case scenario was that you'd have enough money to live a comfortable life, to get all the therapy and whatnot you needed and would need. And we got a bundle with that court case," her father said grimly, remembering. "Why can't I remember the exact sum at the moment? Almost a million? More? I can't seem to —"

"$970,000."

"Yes! That was it. So, you read that. Pretty impressive, wasn't it?" Her father sat back in his chair. "That's not awarded every day, let me tell you, Sophie. Invested it at a good time in the market, too. I can get you the exact figures if you like."

Sophie stifled a frenzied laugh at her father talking to her like he would a client, thinking he would make everything right, that the crux of the problem was that she didn't have the exact, precise amount. Was he forgetting the small fact that the money was for her horrifically shortened life, her increasingly debilitating disease?

Her father was looking expectant.

"Okay." Sophie felt tired beyond belief. "Well, good to have that all in reserve, I guess."

"It certainly doesn't hurt," he agreed.

A long silence settled over the room, each of them lost in their thoughts.

Sophie finally stirred. Her limbs felt stiff, her head ached.

"How are *you* doing, Dad? I read in that case that you —"

"Fine. Under control, under control." He held up a large hand. Keep away. Caution. Danger. Do Not Cross This Line.

"I wish I'd known about your disease, Dad," she said quickly. "We should, you know, help each other."

Their eyes met the sadness and fear in the other's. She reached out her hand, and he grabbed it like a lifeline.

"I'm sorry you found out this way, your mother and I both are. But," he said in a determinedly bright tone, releasing her hand,

"I hope now you feel better. Good to get things out in the open. If you have any questions, don't hesitate to ask, right?"

Again, the mad giggle threatened. *Well, how about: what will happen to us? How long do either of us have before we're not us anymore? There, right off the top, two questions.*

Her father got up stiffly and patted her awkwardly on the shoulder. He turned and started clearing the table.

Such a totally dysfunctional family, she thought. *Neither of us would dream of saying "I love you" even at this terrible time.* She wondered what her father would do if she threw her head back and howled out her pain like a wolf, bared her teeth and sent that primitive streak rampaging through the house. Probably call 911 and let strangers deal with her.

She walked slowly up the stairs. Down the hall, the door to her parents' room was closed. No light under the door; a strip of total blackness.

Sophie hesitated, imagining her mother curled up in bed like a child. Maybe crying, or staring dead-eyed at the wall, remembering.

She felt empty, hollowed of everything but a brief uprush of anger.

I'm the victim here, she thought. *Me.* But she knew that wasn't the whole truth. They were both victims, she and her mother, victimhood passed down like faulty genes. Mariam screwing Elisabeth up, Elisabeth screwing her up.

She went into her room, locking the door.

I am more alone than I've ever been in my entire life. More alone than I was as a little baby during the court case, even.

Because then I didn't even know that I was.

Chapter Nineteen

AFTER A SLEEPLESS NIGHT OBSESSING over all the world's life expectancies and her own, the sun finally, finally coming up felt like a release. She had to get out of her room, out of the house. She stuffed her schoolbooks randomly into her backpack, changed into semi-clean clothes, and scrubbed her face hard with cold water. Hair scraped back, no makeup, she left, slipping silently out the back door.

The grass and trees were damp from night rain, and Sophie breathed deeply the fresh smell of spring in the air. The sun was slanting brilliant, blinding shafts through the leaves.

It all goes on, she thought. *Day after day the sun comes up and goes down. Like it did before I was here, like it will when I'm gone.*

Her feet slowed, and she came to a stop.

Remember the almanac, Sophie? All those dismal life expectancies in places like Afghanistan and Chad and Burkina Faso and Yemen? Those aren't just statistics. They're people — people in all those countries who had sleepless nights and felt despair and smelled spring in the air and wanted to live longer, too.

She forced herself to start walking. Then she walked faster, faster, broke into a half-trot and then a full-on sprint down the street, her backpack banging rhythmically against her back. Finally, she slowed, sweating and panting. There was no outrunning her thoughts, but she felt a little better. She was hungry, ravenous actually. She couldn't remember when she had last eaten. Of course: before reading the case.

Is everything in my life going to be divided into before the case and after it? BC and AC? The play, for example; that was before the case, but now, this morning is after. Before, I was — what was I? Lonely, angry, confused. But also, safe. Innocent. Unknowing. Clueless. Now, what am I? I don't even know. I only know that everything is different.

She caught a bus to the mall, clasping her shaking hands tightly between her knees. McDonald's was open and mercifully empty. She wolfed down an Egg McMuffin meal, extra-large coffee, and sure, why not an extra hash brown? And an apple pie. What the hell did it matter? She sat, pretending to read her book until it was time to head to school.

The day passed in a bleary, silent haze. She tried to appear normal, tried to *be* normal, but then she'd remember. Panic would well up, she would dig her nails or her pen into her palm and endure it, then it would subside.

Here you are, she would tell herself. *Right here, at your desk. Here in this class, with all these people you know.* But she felt so alone, utterly, utterly isolated, like the one person stranded on the lip of an abyss with everyone else on the other side. They were all before the case; she was after. And she couldn't tell anybody. What she now knew was too big, too new, too raw, too scary. She snapped at Lucy and Wayne, neither of whom deserved it. She saw Ms. Linden and Fiona look at each other and shrug and hated them both. That they could talk and move and *laugh*, like everything was just fine, perfectly normal! Everyone in the Op-Shop gave her a wide berth.

She got home after school, kicked off her boots, and opened the Harry Potter cupboard under the stairs. She grabbed a Coke and a bag of chips from her private stash behind her father's old golf clubs and tennis rackets, catching the familiar whiff of dust and stale sweat. As she straightened up, she saw the cushion and flashlight still there from her long hours of reading when she was in grade school.

She teared up, thinking of that little girl who towered over everyone else in fifth grade, hunching, skulking, hiding herself away, escaping into her book-worlds, praying for that letter to Hogwarts. The girl who hadn't even felt worthy of her room upstairs.

Sophie slammed the closet door, turned to the living room, and froze.

Mariam. Curled up in a chair. Mariam, reading, huddled under Sophie's winter coat, looking cold and old, old, old.

"What are you doing here?" Sophie demanded. She choked down the feeling she always got with Mariam of being too big, clumsy, sloppy, awkward, inferior. It was wrong that she'd been made to feel that way all those years. *That* was wrongful. She knew the truth now. She knew what they all knew. She didn't owe anybody anything. She was everybody's equal.

In a strange way, she was free. She felt a rush of exhilaration at the thought.

Mariam glanced up and she shrugged, that slight, one-shoul-dered, European squirm. Indifference, indolence, arrogance. Her eyes dropped to her book.

"Hey, I'm *talking* to you," Sophie said. Mariam's eyes flew up in surprise, locked on Sophie's. She slowly shut her book.

"Well, well. So: talk."

Sophie sat on the edge of the couch, her elbows on her knees, her hands locked together.

"That's my coat." The words were out before Sophie could stop them. Childish. But she couldn't bear the thought of Mariam touching her things, leaving that Chanel No. 5 smell on them. The perfume was like an embodiment of Mariam; Sophie had always loathed it.

"I was cold. This house is frigid. Oh, for Christ's sake, here, take it." She flung the black parka at Sophie. It waved its arms wildly and fell in a crumpled heap in the middle of the room between them. *Childish*, Sophie thought. *God, please don't let me be like her.* "Was that what you wanted to talk about? That spectacularly stylish coat?" The last words were drawled out ironically, as though this was all too boring for words.

"I know everything," Sophie said. "Everything." Mariam regarded her seriously. For once in her life, for maybe the first time in her life, Sophie had Mariam's full attention. Mariam nodded slowly, looking away.

"Good. You should. You should have known it all sooner, in my opinion. Who told you? Don't tell me: your father." She answered the question right after she asked it, shaking her head.

The implied contempt of her mother enraged Sophie. Her whole life she'd watched Mariam belittle her mother, guiltily grateful that she herself wasn't the target. Elisabeth was spineless. Wishy-washy. Elisabeth was tiresome and emotional. She was unattractive, she tried too hard, she lacked panache. She was, crime of all crimes, unoriginal, lacked creativity, common. Sophie had heard it all; the calculated abuse made her own distant, unemotional relationship with her mother look like a gushy Hallmark card.

But Mariam's right on this one. Mom didn't tell me. Neither of them did.

Mariam showed no sympathy. No compassion. Not even much curiosity. *We might be talking about what we're having for dinner*, Sophie thought. *Or the weather forecast.*

"No, I found it when I was searching *your* name in the legal database. And in the midst of your many, many legal battles, I found *my* case."

Mariam waved away her legal battles with a wave of a bony, blue-veined hand.

"*Your* case was the real bitch," Mariam said flatly. "'Wrongful' something." She frowned, and Sophie let her struggle. "What was it? 'Wrongful life' or 'wrongful birth'? Both such desiccating, absurd terms. I loathe legal terminology, anything legal actually. 'The law is a ass.' Bumble. *Oliver Twist.*"

"I don't give a shit about what Dickens had to say about it. I don't honestly give a shit what *you* have to say about it." It felt incredible being able to talk to Mariam like this. "You are nothing to me. *Nothing.*"

Mariam looked at her with that inscrutable face, those black, dead eyes.

"I want to know about Mom's abortion. When she was a teenager," Sophie blurted. Why? Why had she started with that? Maybe because it was easier, not about her, something other than her almost-aborted story, her disability, her early death. Mariam stirred.

"What does that squalid little episode matter? Some pathetic encounter Elisabeth had with some boy. How do these things ever start? Elisabeth fancied she was desperately, tragically in love." The mocking voice deepened, ridiculing even the love her mother had felt for someone. *God knows she needed to find love somewhere,* Sophie thought, *when she'd had Mariam to come home to.* Sophie felt a fleeting interest in her mother's desperate, tragic love affair. She'd been about Sophie's age. *Love can be desperate at my age,* Sophie thought, thinking of Theo's brother Calvin. *Who had mom's Calvin been? Did she think of him still? Did she feel that way about Dad, or had he been someone she settled for?*

"So, you were around? You hadn't dumped her on your mother to raise yet?"

"Oh, I had," said Mariam, using her disconcerting trick of readily admitting her faults. Sophie had heard it before, seen it work a dozen times. If, say, you tell everyone what an atrocious mother you were, they suspect hyperbole, they think it's charming self-deprecation, they soften toward you, they commiserate. When really, Sophie thought, they should take Mariam at face value. She *had* been an atrocious mother. People should have hardened toward her, condemned her. The artistic genius trump card was always in the background, though, waiting to be played at just the right moment.

"I was just in town for a weekend when the shit hit the fan," Mariam continued. "I had no idea Elisabeth even had a boyfriend. Can you imagine what kind of man … anyway, he was just a boy. Just an average boy. All nose and spots. A nobody. And the old lady had *no idea* what to do. Hand wringing like some sort of Victorian companion. Christ. Obviously, an abortion was the only option."

"Was it? Because you weren't going to be the granny getting dumped with a kid like your mom was? Did you think of Mom? Did you even ask her?"

"You think your low opinion of me hurts, Sophronia?" Mariam asked with a small smile. "You think it cuts me to the quick? It's no more than I know of myself, so you can save your insults. They're nothing to me."

"Nothing to nothing. A heart-to-heart with my dear old gran." Sophie smiled bitterly.

"Maybe we share more than I thought," Mariam said, looking at Sophie in assessment.

"We share *nothing!*"

"All right, all right. I told your mother she should have an abortion then," she paused, "just as I told her she should have aborted you."

Sophie flinched. Such a casual knife-twist.

"Nice. Good. We're not pulling any punches here, hey? You told her this after she found out about my disability, you mean? But I was born already —"

"No, before. Early in the pregnancy. Nothing to do with your ... condition." Mariam stretched her legs. "No, Elisabeth and Michael didn't want children. They weren't parent-types. God knows who is, really. Anyway, I didn't think the marriage would last."

Sophie sat, stunned. At least she knew where she stood. Mariam would have killed her outright. Mom and Dad, at least, would have wanted to kill her only because she was defective.

Somehow this is not making me feel a whole lot better. We're racking up the numbers on the people-wanting-me-dead list.

"Wow. Okay. So, when she went through with the pregnancy, when she had had me, that sure must have sucked for you, hey?"

Mariam regarded her steadily.

"Elisabeth struck out on her own on that one. Surprised me. Showed a bit of spine, but of course she got it wrong. She always does. Look where it got her."

"It got her me."

"And your condition. Would you honestly, truthfully choose to bear a disabled baby, Sophronia?"

"I wouldn't *kill* it, if that's what you mean."

Mariam dismissed this with a withering glance.

"I've always loathed imperfection," Mariam said in a musing tone, as if Sophie hadn't spoken, as if she was talking to herself. She looked out the front window. "Maybe that's why my marriages all failed. Imperfect, all of them, because people so often are imperfect. And Elisabeth — so weak, like her father. And you." She turned those black, hooded eyes on Sophie. "You looked so normal, so healthy." There was a hint of accusation there, as though Sophie had tricked them all. "Yet inside, *inside*, there was a taint. Right in your cells. Inside this normal-looking baby." Mariam shook her head, a slight shudder running through her body.

Is that why she couldn't remember Mariam ever hugging her, ever even touching her? Revulsion? Disgust?

"God, I can't imagine how you'd have treated me if I had looked abnormal, if my … disability was right out there," Sophie said, barking out a sarcastic laugh. "If I'd looked like *Abomination*, say."

Mariam, who had been about to say something, froze, her mouth slightly open, her eyes wary. The silence lengthened oddly, disturbingly.

Sophie's heart started to pound, a slow, liquid thrum. They stared at each other, grandmother at granddaughter, old gray eyes locked on young gray ones.

Sophie was remembering. She was remembering Mariam's tight, angry face at the play before she'd slammed out of the classroom. She was remembering Mariam's question afterwards: *Have you never wondered when Abomination was written?* She was remembering her mother and father shutting Mariam down, saying they'd tell her when they were ready. The images snaked through Sophie's mind, flashed bright, floated, and settled into a pattern.

"When did you write *Abomination*?" Sophie whispered. Her throat felt dry. "It was published in 2004, but when did you *write* it?"

Mariam was silent, twisting a big silver ring around her bony finger.

What did it matter? Why did she care? Why this need to know? Stand up, go, just *leave*.

"*When*?"

"When, when?" Mariam hissed. "You want to know everything? Everything?" She looked angry, fierce. She grabbed her Scotch, downed it, and slammed the heavy glass onto the side table. "I wrote that story just after you were born," she said brutally and watched the dawning realization on Sophie's face.

Sophie got up and turned sharply away, blundering into the stair railing, stumbling up the stairs.

More truth.

One more shining, destructive truth.

Abomination is me.

Chapter Twenty

"HI, MRS. SILVA. THEO HERE?" Sophie, on the Silvas' doorstep, called through the screen door.

Because the little shit isn't texting me back because I didn't text him back and I desperately need to talk to him because he's the only person in this whole wide world I can bear right now.

She hoped she didn't look as profoundly weird as she felt. Floating, nightmarish. She tried a shaky smile. Her left eyelid twitched.

"Hi Ronny. Come in, in, in, and shut that door. He's *here*, but …" Mrs. Silva made a harassed face, held out her hands, miming warding something off. "Crap, he's in a bad mood! Like, a real stinker, you know? Warning you." She shook her head, her dangly earrings dancing.

Sophie slipped in the door.

"Maybe I'll go down and talk to him. He's downstairs?"

Mrs. Silva nodded. "Brave girl. Good luck. Chili if you want it later."

"Hi, Ronny." A quiet voice startled her as she walked through the living room.

"Jeez, you scared me, Mr. Silva! Didn't see you. Just gonna say hi to Theo," she pointed at the ground. Downstairs.

Mr. Silva was sitting in an old easy chair, a thick book in one hand. *He probably read more than both of her parents combined,* Sophie thought. Stacks of books everywhere. A big, quiet guy with a slow way of smiling and talking, often sitting unnoticed in a chair somewhere. Like a large cat that people lived around.

"Ah. Good luck." He folded his book, one finger keeping his place. "Everything all right, Ronny?" he asked. "You look a little rattled."

Sophie looked down, swallowed, and nodded her head quickly, not trusting herself to speak. At this mild expression of concern tears had rushed to her eyes. Either she bawled out everything to this poor, unsuspecting man or she stumbled her way to the basement stairs.

She stumbled her way to the stairs.

She dumped her backpack, slid down the slide, and crashed into the basement. Figures it would be a spectacularly painful landing today, when things were going so well. Rubbing her aching knees, she staggered over to the Theo/Calvin quadrant. Calvin wasn't there, and strangely, this fact brought intense relief rather than the familiar jolt of disappointment.

Theo was lying on his back, one arm behind his head, his eyes closed, headphones on. It was like watching him when he was asleep — he looked removed, distant, vulnerable, young. Sophie stared down at his long, curling lashes, his crooked nose, full lips, the familiar planes of his face. The familiar face that was somehow strange in the dim light. She realized she almost never saw Theo *still*. Theo was action, movement, voice, laughter. She couldn't bear this serious, withdrawn stranger.

"Theo," she said. "*Theo*."

She touched his arm and he startled. He ripped off his headphones angrily.

"*Jesus*, Ronny! Heart attack here. What're you *lurking* for? I told everybody I wanted to be alone. *Not* a good time, buddy."

"Sorry, I just wanted to talk. It's okay. We don't have to. Forget it."

Theo sighed.

"Look, I'm in a shit mood, and I don't want to get up, but I *also* don't want to be all craning my neck to look up at you, okay?" He slid over, and she crawled in gratefully, lying back on a spot still warm from him, beside him on the single bed. They both looked at the ceiling, a mesh of pipes and electrical lines and wooden beams.

"So: talk."

"You can listen to your music if you want to, Theo. I'll just lie here. This is good."

"Ronny. You didn't come over to lie on a lumpy old bed." Theo sounded depressed. Preoccupied.

"I — you weren't texting me back. I got worried." *Plus, I'm dying, Theo. Dying.*

He lifted his phone, looked at it, dropped it back down.

"Yep, there you are. Sorry. You want me to read them now?"

"No." What *did* she want? She needed to talk, but she also definitely wasn't ready to talk. She just needed to not feel so desperately alone. She needed to feel there was at least one other person in the whole universe who knew her and cared.

But she hadn't even come to terms with the whole disability thing. She shied away from even thinking about it. It was too huge, the extent of it, the *meaning* of it. All her problems, everything she needed to talk about, hinged on it. Not telling him about the disability meant that she couldn't tell him about the case. There was almost nothing she could tell him.

"I'm Abomination," she blurted. Apparently, she could tell him that. Who knew?

"What?" He turned his head to look at her. "You're what?"

"I'm Abomination. That character in Mariam's story."

"The faceless chick in the play? Isn't that *over*?" Theo sounded bored.

"No, I'm *actually* Abomination."

"You keep saying that but what the fuck does that mean?" Theo said irritably. "How can you *be* Abomination?"

"She based that character on me. She wrote it because of me. She told me."

He blinked at her, taken aback. He had not been expecting that, she thought.

Silence, both of them staring up at the ceiling again.

"Man," said Theo. "That is one evil granny you got. But it doesn't make *sense*, Ronny. Seems to me you got a *face* there, pal." He reached over and clumsily patted her face, pinching her nose, pulling her upper lip, grabbing her left ear. She batted his hand away. "Yep, face, right there." He grabbed her hand and held it up between them. "And proof: fingers. Nice fingers. Right here."

Sophie held his hand tight.

And oh, dear lord, I'm only telling you half the truth because I can't bear the thought of talking about this disease. I can't even face it in my own mind. What would you say, Theo? Would our whole friendship dissolve into pity? You'd be kind, wouldn't you, Theo? Or would you be like Mariam and be repulsed?

"God damn," Theo said to the ceiling. "I can't remember that story almost at all, like practically nothing, except that I hated it. All that useless, flowery language, the *flying*, that God-thing, the Slippery Friend —"

"*Shadowy* Friend." Sophie laughed for the first time in days.

"Yeah, Slithery Friend, all that shit. Symbolism. Allegory. The whole shebang. Oh, who *cares* if your bitch of a granny had some twisted reason for writing that? I don't. Do you?"

"Mmm, I *did* before I talked to you."

"Look, you're a good writer, Ronny. Like, really good. That essay you wrote for me that I got an A on? That was gold." Theo turned to face her excitedly. "So, here's what you do: you go write something mean *about her*! Some long, obscure play or novel or whatever, only way better than her shit, with a main character named *Marian Hale* or something (see what I'm doing? Lawyers, right?). Call it ... lemme think ... *Atrocity*. No, *Obscenity*! No, *Monstrosity*! There: gave you three titles in, like, two seconds. Why am I not writing this?"

He smiled over at her, watching her laugh.

"Ronny, you're the only one who laughs at my jokes. Literally, the only person."

"Oh, my God, Theo," Sophie said, wiping her eyes. "That's so funny. You have no idea how much I needed that. *Monstrosity* ..." She shuddered into another laughing fit, "that's my favorite. That is just brilliant."

"Well, good. That's me, good for a laugh." He flopped onto his back with a sigh.

She turned her head, studying his profile. "So. Tell me your stuff. What's going on?"

"Nah."

"C'mon. I'm frigging *Abomination*. I just unloaded on you. Tell me."

"Ronny, I'm better at being the tellee not the teller. Because when I'm the teller, all I can think about is how pathetic I am."

"You're not pathetic, Theo," Sophie said automatically.

"That's just it. Yes, I am! I am so pathetic you have no idea. That Lauren I liked for a while, who I was telling you about before? She was using me to get to Calvin."

"*Bitch.*"

"Seriously, Ronny. What is that? The fourth girl to do that?" Sophie shifted uncomfortably. She had never done that. If Calvin was here, it was a bonus. She came to see Theo. Her best friend.

"Which actually makes me kind of hate him," he said, "even though it's not technically his fault. He doesn't even notice, which is also a problem. It's like when he's around, I become totally invisible. To everybody."

"Not to me, Theo." She squeezed his hand. "There you are. Right there. I'm sorry, Theo."

"And you know what, Ronny? Since you're listening, since you're the only person who ever *listens* to me, I'm sick of this house, I'm sick of this family, I'm sick of school, I'm sick of this stupid basement where there's no *privacy*, and I'm sick of this fucking hard, lumpy bed." Theo banged his fist down on the mattress. "Sick of everything."

"Which is why you wanted to go to — where was it? Senegal? Vietnam?"

"Anywhere."

"Oh, yeah. Minnesota. That was on the list."

"Sure. Why not? I liked *Fargo.*"

"North Dakota, on the border. Whatever."

Side by side, they debated places to go, arguing, suggesting, laughing, discarding, until it grew dark in the basement.

"Tell me everywhere else you want to go," Sophie said. "Start with, say, Europe."

Stay with me, your shoulder against mine, don't get up, don't stop talking. I don't feel cold and scared and alone when you're with me. I want to stay here with you in this paradise of a basement, on this wonderful, lumpy, hard bed forever.

"I guess maybe Greece, Italy, Spain. Maybe France. Not Latvia, Lithuania, or Estonia. Is that even Europe? Anyway, no desire to go to any of those. Did a report on them. Fish and vodka. Maybe Norway. Finland. Sweden. I'm all about the food court at Ikea ..."

When he ran out of Europe, she prompted him with Africa, Asia, then South America.

As Theo explored all the places he wanted to go, embellishing, galloping continent to continent, throwing out absurd ideas, Sophie smiled up into the darkness. Tears slipped silently from the corners of her eyes into her hair. She felt his arm move, elbow, hip, knee, foot bumping against hers as he laughed and moved and gestured.

Theo was on the beach in Argentina, considering Colombia, weighing the risks of Rio de Janeiro, but for Sophie, in this moment, right now, there was no place in the world she'd rather be than here.

Chapter Twenty-One

SOPHIE HAD READ *GAYLE-ST. JOHN v. Lavoie* six times now, every night, mostly wrapped in a blanket huddled on the couch in the middle of the night. She didn't know why she felt such a compulsion to read it. It scared the hell out of her. But she did. It was the objectivity of it that was both soothing and frightening. Nobody pulling any punches, nobody trying to soften things. Total strangers looking at a situation, discussing it openly, dragging even the horrible things into the light.

She imagined Cutcheon J. looking over his reading glasses at a neurotic woman and her pushy husband arguing strongly that they should have been able to abort their only baby. What did he think of them? Not much, she guessed. That came through in the judgment, a feeling of doing his duty by the law, doing his duty by this baby, in spite of the unsympathetic appellants.

Sophie felt sorry for Dr. Lavoie and the ordeal her parents put him through. He was an old man then, probably very old or dead by now. She developed an irrational hatred of Dr. Strickland, the case's medical expert on Juvenile Huntington's Disease, as though his uncompromising, clinical testimony was rooted in malice or spite. As though he hatched the disease in a lab and syringed it into her newborn self. Even his name repelled her. Strickland.

Stricken. Strike. Struck. She aligned Dr. Strickland with her parents. She and Cutcheon J. were on one side, her parents and Dr. Strickland were on the other.

Cutcheon J. was a thoughtful judge, a sensitive man. Maybe like the grandfather she never really had. Mariam's rotating roster of husbands and lovers didn't count. They changed so frequently that no sooner had you learned their names and met them once or twice, they were out, gone, and somebody else was driving her car, showing up for dinner, beside her in a press photo. And none of them had been much interested in the tall, awkward granddaughter.

Her father's parents, the ones who had adopted him as a baby, had always seemed very old and they lived across the country. Sophie had only met them a handful of times before they died within six months of each other, first her grandmother, then her grandfather. She remembered the fussy guest room she and her parents had had to share, the prominent crucifix, the faded floral wallpaper, homemade jam, her grandfather nudging her shoulder to offer her a peppermint. And her father and mother's irritation with them, their desperation to be gone.

No, it was Cutcheon J. who was her first real friend, her substitute grandfather. Her ally, her defender, after her parents abdicated that position. How had he seen her, the baby who was the subject of the case, she wondered. Had he met her? Did they bring her into court? Had she been introduced to the court as evidence, as an exhibit? She wouldn't have put that past her parents. It was pretty clear Cutcheon J. felt badly for the "baby Sophronia."

She'd read one passage from the judgment over and over until she'd practically memorized it:

To characterize this baby's entire existence as a form of harm warranting compensation profoundly denigrates her life and the lives of all those who live with disabilities.

This court, any court, is ill-equipped to answer philosophical questions about the value of a life. Can life, disability, and nonexistence be quantified? Is this baby's life preferable to her never having lived at all? How can we calculate the joy and love a baby, even one subject to a serious disease, brings to a family to offset their pain and suffering? These questions cannot be answered in a court of law. The law of torts, indeed any law at all, pales in comparison to their enormity.

In the terribly lonely reaches of the night, Cutcheon J. loomed large. Sophie began having mental conversations with him. She pictured him as large and friendly, with shaggy gray hair and twinkling blue eyes, always in a long, black judicial-style robe. A slightly archaic, pedantic way of speaking. God-like, but without the anger. Santa, minus the beard and red suit.

Cutcheon J., do you have children? You must. You understand kids so well. How many do you have?

I do, baby Sophronia, I do indeed. Mrs. Cutcheon J. and I have been blessed with four happy children. I can't calculate the joy and love they have brought us.

Or:

I'm scared of this disability, Cutcheon J. I can barely think about it before I shut it right out of my mind. None of us are talking about it, but we can't bury it forever.

Of course not, baby Sophronia. You must face it. Our youngest

*girl has a disability, and we love her all the more for it. She is strong
in spirit, and wise beyond her years. You remind me of her.*

Sophie used Quicklaw to read some other judgments written by Cutcheon J. None of them were as interesting as her case
(in fact, none of them were interesting at all), but she slogged
through them out of loyalty to her friend.

She googled Cutcheon J. and saw that he was still an active
judge, now over seventy, still on the Court of Appeal. He looked
nothing like she'd imagined. Instead, he was small, bald, with
thick, old-style glasses and a lipless slit of a mouth. He appeared
to be scowling in the picture. But maybe, like her mother, he
didn't like having his picture taken. Not photogenic, perhaps.
Maybe he was shy. Poor Cutcheon J.

In her strange state, in the floating world between normalcy
and complete chaos, it seemed completely rational, even natural, to want to meet the judge, her judge. He still heard cases
at the courthouse downtown, he still lived here. He might even
remember her case. She could just thank him, talk to him a little,
it would take no time at all. Courtrooms were open to the public.
She knew this from her father, who often litigated in court and
complained bitterly about the "gawkers" and the school groups
who drifted in and out of the courtrooms.

Sophie skipped school the next day and took the bus downtown, praying that she didn't run into her father. It took a while
because she had to transfer, and then she got off too early and
had to walk six blocks. But she got there eventually and passed
through the metal detectors at the courthouse with all the other
members of the public, lawyers, witnesses, family members,
possible criminals, litigants. She had her backpack thoroughly
searched by the sharp-eyed guard. She checked the schedule on

the TV screen. Cutcheon J. was scheduled to be in Courtroom 221: *Kabesa Energy Corp. v. Ultimenergy Inc.*

Her story, if she needed one, if pressed by somebody official, was that she was doing research for her Legal Studies class. Their assignment was to sit in on a case and do a report on the judicial system to present to class. Totally plausible.

And I pick courtroom 221, thought Sophie, *no matter what kind of case it is.* She found the courtroom, pulled open the heavy door, and sank down in the first available seat. It was a bland room, windowless, airless, beige. Three judges in black robes and long, white collar-things sat at a raised desk behind a wooden partition. A lawyer was "respectfully submitting" some excruciatingly detailed argument on behalf of her client, one oil company that was suing another in a lawsuit about a patented oil field part. It was almost unbelievably boring, full of detailed technical jargon. Sophie watched the judges. One woman, one youngish man, and old Cutcheon J.

He said almost nothing, sitting hunched and still, his head resting on one hand. At one point, Sophie wondered if he was actually asleep. *Tired, Cutcheon J.? Me too. Not been sleeping almost at all. You? Wow, this is paralyzingly boring, hey, Cutcheon J? Not like my case, where you were so interested, so engaged, so passionate.*

The other two judges roused themselves and questioned the lawyer. Cutcheon J. stirred occasionally, glanced up, and wrote down one or two things. Maybe interesting or relevant facts about the case. Maybe just his own ideas, or even doodles. *I do that too, Cutcheon J.*

Sophie dozed and watched him until, in a wave of mutual relief, the court recessed for lunch. Everyone in the courtroom was told to rise, and the judges gathered up their papers and their robes and left through a secret-looking little door behind their desk. Then the courtroom emptied, the lawyers slamming shut their folders, shuffling their papers, packing away their books in their wheeled bags that gave the place the vague feeling of an airport.

What to do now? The guard was jingling his keys, readying to lock the door. Sophie remembered that there was a small park behind the courthouse, with benches and trees. She and Mom had once met Dad there after a case; they had sat talking while she paced the entire square of grass. *If that park is still there*, Sophie thought, *if it hasn't been turned into a parking lot or something, I could sit there and eat my lunch.*

It hadn't changed much. Some benches and a square of grass, much smaller than she remembered. A hedge muffling the busy street to the left. A few lawyers looking at files. Pigeons. A woman crouched behind a young child on the grass, holding the two little hands upraised as if in victory. The toddler staggered, shrieked, fell, picked herself up, and started again. Sophie sat on a bench, realized it was a beautiful day, and lifted her face to the sun.

Breathe. Feel the sun. Just feel. Don't think. Don't think about anything at all.

Finally, she opened her eyes and fished in her backpack for a granola bar. She crumbled a few pieces and tossed them to the birds.

Sophie heard a sharp click behind her, turned, and saw a brass door open at the back of the courthouse. A burly, bored-looking security guard ushered out a small man. The man walked very precisely and purposefully. His voice droned on in a long complaint about the security alarms being updated.

Sophie stared. It was Cutcheon J., carrying a bag of birdseed, sitting down at a bench, tossing seed to the birds. He had a whole flock assembled in the space of thirty seconds.

Good old Cutcheon J. A kind, good man who fed the birds on his lunch break, and who was my very first friend. It's fate that he's here, within twenty feet of me, feeding the same birds.

I need to talk to him.

Sophie stood up, leaving her backpack on the bench. Best not to antagonize the security guard who gave her a long look as she approached. His hand hovered at the opening to his vest.

"Pardon me, Justice Cutcheon?" she said.

The old man looked up sharply, suspiciously.

"If you have anything you need to address to the court," the security guard said, "you talk to the guards at the front desk. Just inside the front doors." He was walking toward her, pointing the way to the front doors.

"Justice Cutcheon," she called, craning to look past the security guard, "I was the baby in a wrongful birth case you decided sixteen years ago! In 2002. Sophronia Gayle-St. John!"

The security guard hesitated.

Please remember me. Please.

Cutcheon J.'s shaky handful of birdseed stilled.

"Gayle-St. John," he said, looking off into the distance. "Ah!" He looked at Sophie triumphantly. "The old doctor and the baby with the wonky genes! Wrongful birth! Bob, it's all right. Not a criminal case." The security guard relaxed.

"Well, let's have a look at you," Cutcheon J. said, one hand scratching at the scaly patches on his bald head. "You were just a wee baby back then. Heavens, you're a tall girl. Big. You must be, what — how old now?"

"Sixteen."

"And what're you, six feet?"

"I'm five ten," Sophie said, momentarily distracted. What did that matter? "*Anyway*, I've finally read the case. I only just found out everything. How my parents went to court. About my, well, my disability. I just … I just wanted to thank you for your very moving and thoughtful judgment."

He barely seemed to register that she was talking.

"You *look* all right. Weren't you supposed to be — oh, I can't remember the disease or defect. Disability! Weren't you supposed to be disabled?"

"What? Well, I am. I *am* disabled."

"You don't look it."

"I am. I have symptoms. Stiff legs, clumsy hands." Was she really supposed to itemize the progression of her disability here, in a park, in the midst of a flock of pecking pigeons?

"Well, we would have checked they were telling the truth at the time. Proof. Can't have people lying about these things. They do lie. Oh yes, they do."

"Ah. *Anyway* —"

"I recall," Cutcheon J. sat back reflectively, putting his finger to his lips, "that we awarded a whack of damages against that old doctor. Well, against his insurance company, let's be honest. Didn't we?"

"He was negligent. You found that he was negligent. And it was for my care," Sophie said defensively. This man felt nothing like the Cutcheon J. of her judgment. He was abrupt to the point of rudeness. Crude. There was no sympathy between them. "*Anyway*, thanks."

"Don't thank *me*!" He laughed. "It's coming back to me now. I had a clerking student at the time. Pretty girl and a smart cookie to boot. What was her name? D-something. Diane? Darlene? Keen as mustard, and wrote the whole damn … well, helped with the writing of that judgment. Between you and me, there I was, a *corporate* lawyer new to the bench, dumped with whomping together a judgment on a messy case like that."

Sophie looked at him with dawning realization. Her father had once raged about the clerking students at the courts, fresh from law school, who did research for the judges and occasionally wrote "draft" judgments. She had thought he was exaggerating, but turns out, he hadn't been.

"Sir," said the security guard in a warning voice, looking down at his shoes. Cutcheon J. glanced at him irritably, his mouth a thin, ugly line.

"In any event, it was a sad case. Sensitive stuff. Needed a woman's touch. We came up with a solid judgment, a *very* solid judgment. Supreme Court refused to hear the appeal! Don't see that kind of case every day."

"No. No, I'm sure you don't." *I wonder how many of us are actually out there. All the wrongful birth kids.*

Cutcheon J. got up and dumped the rest of the seed from his bag.

So, you were not my first friend. Not my friend at all. Some clerking student was, fresh from law school.

A hot flush of rage stained her cheeks.

You fraud.

You liar.

"Well, you look pretty good, all things considered." Cutcheon J. checked his watch. "Good luck to you."

Alison Hughes

She didn't answer. She couldn't.

Sophie watched him walk back to the building. He waited until the security guard held the brass door open for him, and the two disappeared inside the courthouse.

She stared at the pigeons gobbling up the seeds, and envied their simple lives, their brains too small, too preoccupied with the seed in front of them to hold anyone up as a hero, to feel betrayal, to measure the length of their lives, to expect anything at all.

SHE LIED AT THE OFFICE as she signed back into school. Doctor's appointment. She'd considered just going home, going to bed, but the thought of being alone terrified her.

Room 107 was pretty quiet.

"Hey, Sophie," said Lucy. "How's it going? Doctor's appointment?"

She nodded, then said, "Actually, I went to court."

"Court? Jeez, you get arrested? Anything I should know about?" Lucy laughed, but both of them knew she was only half kidding. Her worried eyes gave her away.

"Long story, but no, I didn't get arrested. Where is everybody?" Adnan and Wayne were the only ones in class, both of them sitting at the bank of computers with headphones on.

"Ms. Linden's at the office, Fiona's sick, and Grace is … I think that's what Ms. Linden is trying to find out at the office."

A shriek from Adnan had Lucy scurrying over to the computers. Wayne whipped off his headphones when he sensed the commotion. He saw Sophie and made a beeline for her, a smile lighting up his face.

"Sophie! Are you here now?"

"Here now, Wayne," Sophie said.

"You see the hockey last night? Islanders beat the Rangers five-three. Five-three."

The sport Wayne was probably clinically obsessed with had never seemed less important. Sophie sagged against the wall.

"Wow. Five-three. Lots of goals."

"Lots. Yeah, lots. My dad said it was an upset."

"You and your dad watch the hockey, Wayne? Together, like?"

"Yeah, yeah. My dad, my mom, my brother and ME," said Wayne, elaborately pointing his short arm at his chest.

"Whole family, hey? Sounds fun."

Sophie couldn't remember her parents watching anything with her. She watched series alone in her room. Her mother watched movies on her iPad in bed. Her father hated movies. She smiled at the thought of Wayne's whole family hooting and cheering for their team.

"And pizza sometimes, too. Or burgers. But I love pizza the best."

"Hey, me too."

"Whatsamatter, Sophie?" asked Wayne suddenly. "You look sad." His wide mouth turned down in an exaggerated grimace. He pointed to the corner of his eye. Tears.

Sophie shook her head, not trusting herself to say anything. She looked down at her Doc Martens, blinking rapidly.

"Sophie?" Wayne was crouching down, trying to look in her face. "You need a hug," he announced.

"You're right, Wayne," Sophie said with a watery laugh. "You're such a smart guy. I think I do need a hug."

He folded her in his arms and clutched her tight against his short, thick body. She closed her eyes.

"You're *tall*," he complained, and she obligingly crouched a little.

Wayne. Born different, disabled. Also born loving and open, kind and wise. Intuitive. Giving her a hug when that's what she needed most in the whole world. When that was what she, private and constrained, was least able to ask for, even from her parents, even at the worst time in her life.

Had Wayne's parents found out about his disability before he was born? she wondered. *Had they considered aborting him? Had they been counselled to? Or had he been a surprise?* She couldn't bear the thought of a world without Wayne.

He was rocking slightly, tunelessly humming.

"What are you humming, Wayne?" Sophie asked into his shoulder.

"That song my mom hums to me if I'm sad. If I get my feelings hurt." Sophie ached to hear that Wayne had his feelings hurt, ever. *God help me, it might've been me who hurt them,* Sophie thought miserably. "It's a good one."

"What's it called?"

He pulled away and screwed up his face, trying to remember.

"It's about a baby. 'Huff, little baby, stop that crying …'" He mangled the tune.

Sophie giggled.

"*Hush* little baby, don't you cry?" she sang the line. "That one?"

"That's it!" he said, amazed that she knew his mother's song.

"Wayne!" Lucy called from the computers. She pointed to the door. Wayne's speech pathologist had just come in for his twice-weekly session.

"Sandra! Sandra! I'm here!" Wayne bellowed across the empty room.

"You gotta go," Sophie said, patting his shoulder and pulling away. "Thanks, buddy."

Wayne patted her shoulder back.

"Hush, lil baby. Don't you ever cry."

Chapter Twenty-Two

SOPHIE WAS IN HER BEDROOM, lying on her bed, trying to listen to music. But she wasn't hearing it. She was looking at her hands, holding them out in front of her.

One of Mariam's husbands, the one with the goatee and glasses, had once said her hands were artistic, the "strong hands of a sculptor." She always remembered that. He'd made her feel better about "those big mitts," as Mariam called them.

Now those hands, her hands, looked alien to her. The left thumb twitched. A spasm passed over the back of the right hand. Left thumb twitched again. Left hand shook, then stilled. She watched those hands, Huntington hands, that were not her hands anymore, twitch and jerk involuntarily, fear growing deep within her.

Loss of control over movement, thought, and emotion.

Sophie had, at first, focused on the personal betrayal, the unfairness, the monstrosity of the court case her parents had brought. Blame was comforting, even righteous. But then, she and her parents had hit a wall. After the emotion burned down, after the hurled recriminations and the defensive justifications, there was nothing left to say. They were all exhausted. The court case happened, they initiated it, it was terrible, it was what they thought they had to do, sorry you had to find out like that, end of story.

But it wasn't the end of the story. Sophie realized that a deep, profound fear had been lurking all along, beast-like, behind the anger. And once the anger burned off and settled to a simmer, fear stood, roared, and shook Sophie to her core.

Fear of this disease, fear of the things it would do to her, fear of the independence it would take from her, fear of death. All the other fears she'd ever had seemed puny, laughable in comparison to the enormity of this fear. Public speaking? Spiders? The dark? *Seriously?* If she could have traded her current situation for one where she had to habitually make speeches in a dark room crawling with spiders, she'd have done it in a heartbeat.

This disease was, as Theo would have said had he known about it, "a whole 'nother ball game." There was nobody to blame. Her father hadn't known about his own disease. He'd only been tested after his baby had been diagnosed; the revelation that he had adult Huntington's was another terrible shock, but this one with no convenient doctor to sue. The contents of her father's genes had been as secret to him as Sophie's had been to her.

But now all she could hear were her genes, her body's traitors, directing this discordant finger-trembling, this shaky symphony. She would have to face this disease, and if she couldn't throttle it, she could at least corner it, outwit it, dupe it. Slow it. She had to do everything she could to slow it down.

Buy some precious time for herself, for the things that made her Sophie, for her very own movement, thought, and emotion.

DR. STRICKLAND WAS DARK AND short and wide, with small feet and hands. A bustling, cheerful doctor who clearly favored colorful, conversation-starter ties. Today's tie was covered in pink flamingos. He was nothing like she'd imagined from her readings of the case. In dry, economical court language, he was the most terrifying character in her case. She hadn't even considered what he looked like; he may as well have been the Grim Reaper. "She will lose all faculties. She will die. There is no cure." Casually swinging the scythe in long, destructive sweeps.

Pretty sure he wouldn't have worn the flamingo tie to court, Sophie thought.

When her name was called, she and her mother both rose.

"I'm going in by myself, Mom," she said. She wanted to spare her increasingly frail mother more stress. She wanted to see Dr. Strickland alone. She'd apparently been to see him before, but she didn't remember him. She'd been young; he had been one of a series of appointments.

Sophie sat, arms crossed, listening to him go over her history from their family doctor, the physiotherapist, and occupational therapist.

He was very kind, not at all the monster she'd built him up to be.

"— so, you see, Sophie, up until these relatively recent symptoms, you've done remarkably well. Re*mark*ably well."

"Yeah, I'm a total rock star," Sophie said. She leaned forward, elbows on her knees, hands clasped tightly. "Look, Dr. Strickland, I don't care about my *history*. That's over. What I need to know is *what happens next*? What will happen? Will I lose everything? Will I — what? Not be able to brush my teeth, or recognize my friends, or control my anger or my *bladder*? What? And when? Will I lose my mind tomorrow? Next week? I need answers. I really do. I have to know how much time — how much *real* time I have. Not just how much time I *technically* might have left, lying in a bed, totally dependent on other people. How much of *my* life is left?"

Dr. Strickland sat back in his chair and looked down at his plump, clasped hands. He raised weary eyes.

"The truth is, Sophie, I just don't know," he said. "I'm not lying or shielding you from the truth. I'm being completely honest. Juvenile Huntington's Disease is unique to each child. I can't predict how your disease will play out. I can't answer many of those questions." He spread his hands wide. He looked at her steadily. "What I *can* tell you is that it's in your favor that the disease began to manifest itself reasonably late in childhood. From my reading of events, your symptoms only began in earnest one or two years ago. The stiffness of your legs. The 'clumsy' hands. The difficulties in school. Had they begun when you were much younger, the disease generally would have progressed more rapidly."

He paused. Her breathing quickened.

"I don't, however, want to minimize what you have experienced and ... will increasingly experience, Sophie. The chorea, those involuntary tremors you have noticed, will continue. They will worsen. There is no medication we can give you to slow the progression of the disease," — he leaned forward, suddenly fierce and deadly serious in his flamingo tie — "but let me tell you, we will put together one *hell* of a team to help ease your symptoms."

He listed them off on his fingers: him, family doctor, psychologist, physiotherapist, occupational therapist, dietician, social worker.

Sophie gripped her hands together so tightly they were numb.

"Okay, good, thank you, that's all good," said Sophie with a shaky smile. "But what I need to know is how will it go? What will —" She stopped, struggling to put into words the enormity of what she was asking.

How will I die? When will I die?

"I'm so sorry to have to say this," Dr. Strickland said, "but you've told me you want the truth. You're very brave, you know; many people don't. They just want to run from it."

Well, I would if I could. Not really an option.

Dr. Strickland gave her a long, steady look, full of compassion.

"You will gradually lose the ability to speak clearly, to walk, or do almost any daily tasks without assistance."

Sophie swallowed. Her mouth had completely dried up.

"Daily tasks? What — like making my bed?"

"That, yes. Also, other things. Hopefully many years in the future, you'll need help with eating, getting dressed, going to the washroom, bathing. Eventually, well, eventually you may need twenty-four-hour care. All of this is not pretty, I know. But it's the truth."

"And the truth is that this thing is a total bitch that will destroy me before it kills me," Sophie said, tears running unchecked down her face. When she was younger, lying awake in her room, she would think about the worst ways to die. After thoroughly freaking herself out by running through all the dreadful options, she would settle on shark attack. Or being burnt to death. Toss-up between those two. But right now, those deaths seemed mercifully quick. *Bring on the sharks, flick that lighter.*

Dr. Strickland came around his desk and sat in the chair beside her. Not touching, just sitting, his elbows on his knees, hands clasped. In these parallel postures they both looked at the ground. They looked like teammates on the bench on the losing side of a blowout game.

"I wish I could say things were different, Sophie," he said. "I really do. And remember, research is ongoing, clinical trials, experimental drugs. Who knows what breakthroughs might happen in the next few years?"

The silence lengthened.

"And remember. You'll have a team around you. We'll be there with you."

Sophie nodded, blinking hard, her face crumpling from his kindness.

There was absolutely nothing more to say.

"Okay," Sophie said, getting to her feet, "thanks." That mad giggle bubbled up. *Thanks. Thanks? Thanks so much for all the wonderful news!* But she really did feel grateful. Grateful that he'd been honest, grateful he was kind, grateful he was going to help her fight.

Who knew that Dr. Strickland, not Cutcheon J., was the real friend in her case?

She walked back to the waiting room. Her mother jumped up, her face anxious.

"I should talk to Dr. Strick —" she began.

"No, Mom. Let's just *go*."

"Okay, I'll call him later."

"Or you can just talk to me," Sophie said.

"Right! Right. We'll talk."

"Let's just get to the car."

In the car, her mother turned to her, wordlessly pleading for something, anything. Sophie looked out the window, terrified, hopeless, helplessly inarticulate.

"Fasten your seat belt, Mom," Sophie finally said, not talking about the car. Her voice was all over the place — too high, too loud, sliding from a bitter laugh to a sob. "It's going to be one hell of a bumpy ride."

Her mother groped for her hand and held it tightly. An unfamiliar hand; a birdlike claw, a small pouch of bones. But Sophie's hand clung back, holding on to her mother's hand for dear, dear life.

They sat in the hospital's dim parkade, staring out the windshield at the concrete pillars, the pylons, the elevators, and the people in other, happier, more fixable lives walking to their cars.

Chapter Twenty-Three

SOPHIE SAW CRYSTAL, HER SIX-YEAR-OLD neighbor, playing outside. Desperate to escape her thoughts, she pounded downstairs, irrationally afraid that by the time she got outside Crystal would have gone in. She breathed deeply when she got outside. The late afternoon smelled of sun and wet earth and spring freshness.

Crystal was clearly in a bad mood, arms crossed, kicking at a loose fence board with her boot.

"Hey, Crystal," said Sophie. "What are you doing?"

"Just kicking."

"Why?"

"Because I *want* to," she said aggressively. Hard to argue with that.

"*I* feel like kicking something, too," said Sophie. Crystal looked up quickly at Sophie to see if she was teasing. Apparently satisfied she wasn't, Crystal moved over a few inches to give Sophie a clear shot at the fence board. Sophie smacked it hard.

"Take that, fence!" Sophie cried. Crystal giggled.

"Take that, fence! Take that!" Energized, Crystal renewed her assault.

They hammered, kicking one at a time, then dissolved into a wild frenzy of kicking and laughing.

Take that, Huntington's! Take that!

When the fence had been kicked enough, Sophie offered a piggyback. Crystal's boots were caked with mud that smeared her hands and jeans, but it was a small price to pay for two thin arms around her neck and a little face pressed into the side of her neck.

Sophie waved to Crystal's mother at the window, and let her know through pointed miming that they were going down the street. Maybe Theo would be around.

Sophie tried to do her signature cantering pony, a bouncing, rollicking ride that Crystal loved, but she slid in a patch of mud and almost fell.

"Whoa, horsie!" Crystal screamed, her thin thighs clenching on Sophie's waist.

"Sorry about that," Sophie said. "This old horse better be careful, hey? Got a very special little piggy on my back."

"I'm not special. I'm not. Jayla said, 'you think you're *so* special. Well, you're not.' And she plays with Conner now."

Sophie absorbed the covert viciousness of first graders. She remembered it. Lana Andrews telling the girls not to sit next to Sophie on the reading carpet, so she had to sit back with the boys, especially Martin Sikorski who picked his nose. These are things you remember. Also, mean jokes about being tall, not getting a pink birthday invitation, the sight of friends running away from you, boys mimicking the way you ran, exclusive recess groups, exclusion, period.

"Well, she's not worth playing with, right, Crystal? You should play with people who appreciate you. Who think you're special."

"Nobody does."

"That's not true. I do. And we're playing right now."

"You're big. You're a *big* girl."

"Well, even little kids will see you're special too. And sometimes, Crystal, it's also okay to play all by yourself." She clutched the thin legs tighter. "Remember that."

We're all alone, Crystal. We're so alone.

Get used to it, my little friend.

Chapter Twenty-Four

THAT NIGHT, DESPERATE TO FORGET, to sleep, to not think or feel anything, Sophie shoved the bottle of Scotch they kept for Mariam under her sweater and smuggled it up to her room. It tasted terrible, but she drank until she felt sick, until she passed out. She woke in a panic in the middle of the night with a splitting headache and a heaving stomach, rushed to the bathroom, and threw up. Catching her eye in the mirror as she straightened from washing her face, she almost didn't recognize her reflection: lank hair, dark circles under bloodshot eyes, greenish pallor.

You are pathetic. What were you thinking? Never again. This is not how you are going to spend the rest of the life you have left: addled, bleary, nauseous, fuzzy-tongued, hideous. Defeated.

No.

She scrubbed her face again, hard. Brushed her hair hard. Brushed her teeth.

Back in her bed, she lay and listened to the seconds tick away on the bedside clock. Each one was dog-like, she thought, each one worth seven times a normal, human second. She asked a God she'd long ignored and dismissed what she was supposed to do with the rest of her life.

A one-word response came fast and clear. Was it God? Or herself? The voice in her head said: *Fight.*

It gave her courage. Fighting was positive, it was on-your-feet, at-the-ready. Fighting was something she knew how to do. She seemed to have been doing it all her life, battle after battle after battle.

This disease was her enemy, her defences already breached. Since Sophie had read the decision, even after her appointment with Dr. Strickland, she'd been unable to even google Juvenile Huntington's Disease. It seemed as scary and reckless as opening a box full of live snakes. Her parents didn't bring it up, either. They were wary with her, watching, waiting with unusual consideration, or fear, for her to broach the issue.

It would be her mother double-knocking on the door to her room. Standing there, looking ill and uncertain. *Are you okay? Do you want me to get you anything?* Willing her to say that she was okay, that she didn't need anything. Sophie felt pity mixed with rage. Barking out "I'm *fine*," when she wasn't. When she was crumbling to the ground.

Or her father lurching into the kitchen, trying to talk to her about the news, world events, something supremely useless like the latest home renovation plans.

What on earth is that to me, Dad? To you?

Sometimes, especially with her father, Sophie vividly imagined very different conversations.

"So, how long do you figure you have left, Dad? Like, of living? Will I die before you?"

Or, shrieking, "Why do you fucking even go to work, Dad? You're *dying.*"

Or shaking his shoulders until his head lolled and his teeth rattled. "Wake up, wake *up!*"

Or breaking down completely. "Your stupid genes, your stupid, stupid genes."

But it never happened. They were careful around each other. The disease that was decimating and devastating the lives of two-thirds of the family was never discussed. A dropped pot was picked up, a stumble ignored, a forgotten word or name quietly supplied. Heads turned away from any reminder of the disease; it was felt only in the simmering underneath their skins and in the depth of the silence.

And the elephant in the room, Huntington the Elephant, watched them through its ancient eyes, through its long lashes. It moved room to room with them, silent, sullen, and dumb. It lumbered up the stairs with her, it shambled to school beside her, it blocked the halls. It sat heavily on her chest. And it grew and grew and grew.

Now, here in her room, in the middle of the night, she was ready for a fight. She stared down this disease like an army assessing an enemy. *I want to know your moves, when you will strike, how you fight, how much time I have, what weapons I can possibly use against you. And maybe, just maybe, since my case in 2002, there have been some hopeful medical developments.* She clung to that, even wondering how rigorously Dr. Strickland kept up to date.

She opened her computer, took a deep breath, and for the first time punched the words *Juvenile Huntington's Disease* into the search box. A list of links came up, and she dived in at random, like the first stages of a research project. Just amass information. Read.

She began clicking on websites — Wikipedia, the Mayo Clinic, the Huntington Society. Reading medical journal articles clinically, impartially, notebook open, printer on, highlighter at the ready. Symptoms, confirmation, progression, prognosis; she made a file folder for them all. She read firsthand accounts about coping with the disease, about living with it. She learned that any children she might have had a 50% chance of contracting it from her. *Would she have children? Did she have time to have children?* She was sixteen, nearly seventeen. She'd always assumed she'd have children, but somehow thought she'd make that decision later, much later, like normal people, if she was ever in a relationship.

She read for hours, on a mission, single-minded. A ticking time bomb with a focused desperation for instructions on how to diffuse herself. Printing off information, neatly labeling file folders; it got so that she could read the most horrible statistics, the most jarring first-person accounts of living with the disease, without even flinching. She worked the rest of the night.

One last file folder. Disease: Cure. It was empty. So empty, so empty.

She got up stiffly, flipped through a photo album and selected one of the only pictures she liked of herself. Her, earlier this year, holding a therapy puppy they'd brought to Room 107. The picture was snapped just as the dog reached in to lick her face. She'd squirmed with one eye squinted shut, and she was laughing delightedly. The picture was pure happiness.

She put the picture in the folder. She stroked out Disease: Cure. There was no cure. Any developments there had been were about managing the disease. There was no room for pretending.

She wrote The Future instead. Because, no lie, she still had some kind of future ahead of her.

I'm not going down without a fight, she thought.

She turned her mind to the desperately urgent business of living.

Chapter Twenty-Five

DOORBELL.

In the kitchen, Sophie checked the clock. 11:32 Saturday morning. Theo? Crystal?

She opened the door to two uniformed police officers.

"Hi, is Mrs. Gayle-St. John available?" The female officer took the lead. "We need to speak with her."

"I — uh, sure. Just let me get her. You want to come in?" The police officers came in, politely wiping their boots on the front mat.

Sophie ran up the stairs and down the hall. She burst into her parents' bedroom where her mother was working at her little desk set in the middle of the bay window. She looked up, startled, pulling out her silicone earplugs.

"Mom," she said breathlessly, "there are two cops here wanting to see you. I swear to God, I didn't do anything."

"Police?" Her mother frowned and pulled on her cardigan. Sophie followed her down the stairs. She heard her mother say, "Hello, I'm Elisabeth Gayle-St. John. What can I do for you?"

"Mrs. Gayle-St. John, could we possibly sit down?"

"Oh, God, what is it? Michael, my husband —"

"No, no, this isn't about your husband. Our visit is about your mother." Sophie, sitting on the bottom stair, relaxed. Some shit of Mariam's. *Am I actually so monumentally screwed up that cops on the doorstep for some dumb thing Mariam's done is actually a wildly entertaining, very welcome diversion?*

"My mother?" Sophie couldn't bear seeing her intelligent mother stumble and struggle. "My *mother*?" She seemed to be having difficulties focusing.

"Mom," Sophie said sharply, "*Mariam*. It's about Mariam."

The police officer led her mother into the living room and sat beside her on the couch. Sophie strained to hear what they were saying. The other police officer in the hall tilted his head in the direction of the living room. "You should probably be in there," his head said.

"I can't believe that. No, really, I *can't*. There must be some mistake," her mother was murmuring, shaking her head.

"Mom? What's Mariam done?" Sophie hovered awkwardly.

Her mother looked up at her, her eyes swimming wide and bewildered behind the thick lenses.

"There must be some mistake," she repeated. "This officer is telling me that Mariam took too many *pills*, Sophie, and —"

"And what? She's in the hospital?"

"No, this officer is telling me she's *dead*."

Sophie groped for a chair and sat down. "*What? Killed herself?*" She felt numb, felt nothing. "I don't believe it."

The patient officer, doubtless used to having to convince families that this sort of news was not, in fact, some sick practical joke they liked to pull, explained again. She turned to Sophie.

"You're the deceased's granddaughter?" Sophie nodded. *Mariam.* "*The deceased.*"

"Ms. Gayle was found this morning at 10:05 by a hotel maid

who had entered to make up the room. 911 was called but the deceased had already passed away. Preliminary estimates by the attending physician indicate that she passed away last night. Between six and ten hours before she was found. No foul play is suspected. She left a note."

"She left a note," Sophie's mother repeated. "A note."

Sophie hoped the police weren't reading anything into their reactions. They were both shocked, but dry-eyed. Detached. Unemotional.

Her mother straightened her back, hooked her hands over one knee. "She's a great writer, you know."

Oh, God, Mom, leave it. Just leave it.

"I've heard that," said the police officer, politely. "I'm so sorry for your loss." She waited for a few minutes before saying, "I wonder if you might be able to come and identify the deceased. It will be a very brief visit. She died very peacefully."

"Of course, of course." Sophie's mother looked around her like her purse, her coat, her keys would simply appear when she needed them.

"I'll come, too," Sophie said loudly. "Mom, I'll come with you."

She saw relief flood her mother's face. She was grateful for reinforcements against even a dead Mariam.

"You're welcome to follow us in your own vehicle if you feel able to drive," the officer said, "or you can come with us."

"We'll come with you," said Sophie firmly. Her mother was a terrible driver at the best of times, and she looked shocked and confused now. Sophie didn't have her license yet. Would she ever get it now? The thought flitted through her mind as she grabbed her mom's coat, purse, and keys.

They climbed into the back of the police vehicle.

"Sorry for the arrangements here," apologized the nice police officer. "Cage isn't detachable."

"Haha," yelped Sophie nervously.

"I hope none of the neighbors are looking," muttered her mother.

"They'd hardly think *both* of us would get arrested, Mom. Together. Some joint — what? *Heist*?" Her mother let out an unexpected bark of laughter, and they both dissolved in stress-giggles.

"Stop," whispered her mother, trying to control herself. "What are these officers going to think of us?"

Sophie bit hard on the inside of her cheek, grabbed her mother's hand, and looked out the window as the cruiser swung out of the neighborhood.

"Where are we going, Mom? Where was Mariam even staying?"

"She never told me where she was. Just showed up, then left. Dad drove her back to a house in Lakeside Manor a week ago, but he got the impression that was just for a few nights. So maybe Le Marchand? She hadn't stayed there for a while."

It used to enrage Sophie, this futile speculation her parents always went through when Mariam came to town. Was she staying with friends, with another writer, was she in a relationship, at an exclusive boutique hotel? Today, though, Sophie was grateful that her mother could slip into the old pattern. At least they weren't talking about what they'd find when they got there.

It was, surprisingly, the Riche that they pulled up to. Mariam always said she despised big, ostentatious hotels, so the choice was puzzling. Maybe she'd lied, thought Sophie. Maybe all these years she'd been secretly enjoying plush hotel robes, spas, and champagne.

In the elevator on the way up, Sophie felt her mother's nervousness, saw her hand tremble as she adjusted her glasses. Her own tension was coiling, making it difficult for her to breathe. Mariam, dead, here in this hotel. It seemed impossible, it seemed like this was a dream, like they were dutifully acting their parts in a strange and dreadful play. The elevator stopped. Here, she was here, her body, somewhere on this floor. They walked to a room cordoned off with police tape and another officer outside. Here, in this room.

Room 512, must remember that, thought Sophie. Dad will ask. *Dad.* They hadn't thought to call him.

"Mom, should we call Dad?" Sophie whispered. She was shocked at how gray and ill her mother looked.

"No. Oh, no. He doesn't need this right now. Neither do you. I think you should wait here in the hall."

"That would be worse, Mom. Way worse. I'll just imagine more horrible stuff." Mariam clenched in spasms of agony, contorted, teeth bared, her face livid, blotchy, bloated. Eyes bulging, blood everywhere. "Please. Oh, God, Mom, *please*. Let's just do this together."

"Shhh, okay, if you think ... if you don't think ..."

Their officers conferred with the officer at the door, who unlocked it and let them in.

A beautiful room, light and airy in blues and whites, a view over the park. They walked through a small, stale-smelling sitting room littered with stacks of books, papers, notebooks, a laptop, empty bottles, takeout containers, clothes. Mariam's trail of crumbs.

They turned into the bedroom and Sophie's mother stopped so suddenly in front of her that she bumped into her.

A figure lay in the center of the bed, as small and slight as a child under the heavy covers. She was on her back, her long dark hair streaming out on either side of her head, disarrayed slightly. *From the maid, trying to shake her awake,* Sophie thought. *Or the doctor.*

Sophie came closer. Mariam's face was calm, even serene, no trace of the usual bitter twist to the mouth. The hard, angry eyes were closed, her mouth slightly open. She looked old, ancient. Sophie saw with a shock that there was a thin strip of pure white hair on either side of her middle part; *fastidious Mariam hadn't even bothered to touch up the roots,* Sophie thought. The small, bony hands — like her mother's hands — were on top of the covers, folded one on the other. Like a picture of a saint, or a body in a coffin.

Mariam had been energy, bitterness, intensity, rage. A primitive streak of a person, slash-and-burning her tornado way through the world. With all that gone, extinguished, her little shell of a body was almost pathetic. *She looks,* Sophie thought, *like a Mariam-dummy, a statue carved of pale marble, a wax prop for a play.* The Death of Mariam Gayle. The stage being set, she half expected to hear Mariam's gravelly laugh from the other room, mocking them for being duped into believing she was dead. It would take a long time to get over Mariam and everything she'd done to them.

So little, so harmless now. Will I look that peaceful when I die? Sophie felt cold right through thinking about it. It's one thing to contemplate the death of an old person. It's another big leap to think about your own death. Suddenly, absurdly, she felt blisteringly angry at Mariam — angry and jealous that she got seventy-one years, and even chose to throw the rest of it away.

Glutton. Thief. Coward.

And me? I get fifteen more years at most. Maybe way less. Tears welled up in Sophie's eyes at the unfairness of it all.

There were bottles of pills on the nightstand. A book. A bottle, mostly empty, of Scotch.

"Yes, that is my mother," said Elisabeth loudly, startling Sophie. She had almost forgotten that they were here to identify Mariam. She'd thought her mother was going to launch into a dramatic monologue about how great Mariam had been. "That is Mariam Gayle."

"Thank you, Mrs. Gayle-St. John. Do you want a moment alone with her?"

Her mother stared at the officer, her hand going to her throat.

"Oh, no. No, no." She backed away, afraid of Mariam still.

"You said she left a note," Sophie said. "Is it for us?"

"It's not actually addressed to anyone," said the police officer, handing Sophie's mother the page of paper. "But, as next of kin, we're presuming it is directed to you. We'll ensure all her personal effects are packaged up and sent to you. There was this found among the papers as well, which may have some bearing on the incident." The incident? *The suicide, you mean*, Sophie thought. *Why are we all avoiding the word?*

"This" was a report from a specialist. Mariam Gayle, age seventy-one, confirmation of a diagnosis of Parkinson's disease. Dated three days ago.

"She never told me," said Sophie's mother. Then, more bitterly, "She never told me anything."

Finally, it all made sense. *No kidding that doctor's report* may *have had some bearing on the incident*, Sophie thought. *Mariam couldn't have borne a debilitating disease. She took the easy way out.*

Coward.

Sophie pulled her mother into the sitting room, and they sat on the couch together and read the last words Mariam Gayle ever wrote.

I am weary of this life. It holds no further mysteries for me.
    I have explored it to the depth and breadth and height my soul can reach.

("Elizabeth Barrett Browning," murmured her mother. "From 'How Do I Love Thee?'" *Full marks, there, English prof,* thought Sophie. *Only, Mariam was talking about herself, of course. There was no "thee" with Mariam. Only "me."*)

I have left my mark.
    I refuse to waste away. I will not diminish. I choose another, bolder path.
    No regret. No mourning.
    Leave me be.

The spidery handwriting stopped.

Sophie snatched the paper from her mother and turned it over. Nothing on the back. That was it.

"So powerful," her mother said, sitting back.

"Oh, for fuck's *sake.*"

"Sophie —"

"No, seriously, Mom. Powerful? *Powerful*? This isn't a piece of literature, you know. God, she doesn't even know how to be a human being in a suicide note! No message for you, her only daughter, who has to deal with this, now, on top of … well, everything else. No 'good luck with all that, Liz'! No apology to me for using me for *Abomination* when I was only a little baby! No 'sorry I was such a complete and utter bitch my whole life, folks.' Nope. No regrets. Unreal."

"You know about *Abomination*? You didn't tell me."

"Mariam told me. She *wanted* to tell me, Mom."

"That's awful." Her mother shook her head. "I suspected, but she never really told me. I saw how she reacted to your play, though. When you came out in that fencing mask. I'm sorry. She's — she was —" Her hands fluttered uselessly.

"Mariam. She was Mariam, Mom, the most selfish person either of us will ever know. God. This *note*, written with an eye to the media, no doubt, is all *I, I, I,* and *me, me, me.*"

Her mother rubbed her hands over her tired eyes.

"We'll never understand all this, Mom," Sophie said. "But at least we're free. We're free of her."

Her mother looked at her wonderingly.

"I suppose we are."

Sophie stood up, pulled her mother up.

"Do they need us for anything else? I've had enough of Mariam. And death."

Chapter Twenty-Six

LEAVE ME BE WAS THE headline emblazoned on papers across the country when Mariam's last note was somehow leaked to the press.

"I'm sure it was Addison," her mother said. The unqualified colleague at the English department, Sophie remembered. She'd been over once for dinner. All Sophie could remember were her prominent, rodential front teeth that didn't seem to fit behind her lips, ever. "She begged to see the note, and we had a long discussion about whether it belonged in the public domain, archived with Mariam's works." Sophie stared at her mother. People who worked at universities actually talked like that? "Anyway, Dr. Schaefer came to the door, I was distracted, and I'm sure Addison snapped a photo of it. I mean, who else could it be?"

"Did you show it to Dr. Schaefer?"

Her mother hesitated. "I did. He and Mariam were … very close at one time."

"I did give our senior partner just a little peek at it," said Sophie's father. "From that pic on my phone. Old Jerome. Very literary old gent. Adored Mariam. And Trenton. But that's *it*."

"Wow, you've both been shopping around Mariam's suicide note?" Sophie said.

"Sophie." Her mother's lips tightened.

"So, it's really no big surprise that it got out. Whatever. It's not like she wrote it for us."

There were other headlines: "Famous Last Words," "No Mysteries Left," and "Mariam Gayle Exits on her Own Terms." And those were only the ones Sophie could stomach. The ones without the words *great, towering genius, national treasure, icon,* and *irreplaceable.*

Mariam was everywhere — photo essays, retrospectives of her life and loves, her fights and feuds, planned reprintings of her novels, her collected works. Prominent writers expressed sadness, horror, gratitude, recounted her "dry and cutting wit," her "biting, pithy prose." Artists discussed the last time they'd spoken with her, reading into their conversations the seeds of her death. There was talk of a posthumous Nobel Prize in Literature for her latest collection of short stories.

Sophie's father lurked by the front window, twitching the curtain and striding to the door to scatter the reporters that came by hoping for an exclusive interview.

"Vultures," he muttered.

But his eyes were bright and there was a spring in his step. The mood in the house had improved immeasurably with Mariam's death. There was a sense of release, of lightness, of importance, an odd kind of camaraderie. It was, Sophie thought, in a seriously twisted way, precisely the diversion they had needed from their bleak lives, and all three of them embraced it gratefully. She felt it herself. She grabbed feverishly, almost indecently, at this reprieve from thinking about her own mortality.

Reporters camping out on the front walk, international media attention, flowers coming in, phones ringing, messages, interviews, hoopla, commotion. All welcome, so welcome; a bright line of interest underscored the inevitable exhaustion, irritation, and annoyance.

Sophie scrolled through the news reports idly, calling out details to her parents.

"Picture of Mariam holding you as a baby, Mom. BBC News."

"Let me see." Her mother trotted over, leaning on Sophie's shoulder. "Oh, that one. They've spelled my name wrong."

"Add it to the file, will you?" called her father. Always the lawyer, he was keeping a record of the media coverage "for defamation purposes."

Her mother, looking pinched, pale, and nervous, wearing a terribly unflattering mustard yellow turtleneck, did a national television interview.

"You can't possibly say 'no' to *The Query*," she'd said. Sophie watched the interview, squirming at the interviewer's fawning attitude. How did it feel to have had a "literary rock star" for a mother? "Well, she certainly wasn't like other mothers." Sophie's mother's tight, dutiful smile covered up all the years of neglect and abuse. Sophie felt profound sympathy for her mother. The mere fact of having given birth to her hadn't made Mariam a mother.

What, in her opinion, was Mariam's greatest legacy? How does the literary world rebound from such a loss? Were there works in progress? Would Elisabeth write a biography of her mother? On and on and on.

A reporter even approached Sophie on her way home from school. She was young, frizzy red hair, open face. But Sophie had been coached by her tight-lipped parents not to divulge anything about Mariam. They were terrified of what she would say. Sophie acquiesced not for them or for Mariam, but because she didn't know if, once she started, she would be able to stop.

But the reporter got a scoop from Ms. Linden. Yes, they had performed the play version of *Abomination*, and yes, they had had the honor of Mariam's presence at the production. Such a profound piece of work. Yes, she had just had a few, a very few words with Ms. Gayle. She had been passionate about the production, full of artistic intensity.

How many euphemisms can people invent for Mariam, Sophie wondered. The headline in the local paper had been: "Famed Writer Supports Local High School Play."

Death sanitizes everything, Sophie realized. In the aftermath of her death, all of Mariam's sharp edges were smoothed over, all her faults and flaws minimized, her good writing exaggeratedly venerated, her bad writing left quietly uncriticized. She hadn't been a selfish, narcissistic, mean, rude bitch, Sophie realized. All that was gone. Sophie didn't recognize the person that emerged. Some kind of saint/sage/prophet/earth mother. Whoever that person was, it sure wasn't Mariam.

"It's like there's no objective *truth* with a dead person," she said to Theo over coffee. Theo was loving this media circus and was gleefully messing with the press. Two reporters had showed up at Parthenon Greek Eats after a "tip" that the manager was Mariam's half-brother.

"Well, Ronny, there are many versions of 'truth.' Just kidding. That's the kind of shit dumb people say. Or liars."

"*Yes*. Like, *I* know who she was, what she was like. She was a total narcissist."

"See, right there, nobody's gonna know what that means, so."

"Okay, hellaciously self-centered then. A monster."

"Monster is more relatable. Hey, —" he sat straighter in his chair "— maybe the time is ripe for you to write that Atrocity-Monstrosity story about her!"

"She only died a week ago, Theo. Don't you think that might be —"

"If you were going to say, 'a wicked-smart business decision,' you'd be totally right! People'd jump all over that shit right now that she's in the news."

"I was going to say, 'a little insensitive.'"

"Like the old hag cared about sensitivity. Who was it she based *Abomination* on?" He pondered elaborately, eyes to the ceiling. "Oh, yeah, it was you." He tilted his head. "Why you, by the way? We've established a face and fingers. Never seen you fly, but maybe you do that alone in your room. Ronny up there cracking her head on the ceiling, bouncing off the walls."

"Shut up. I ... I don't know. Mariam was profoundly weird."

Perfect opportunity right here to tell Theo everything.

No, I can't. I can't tell you yet. It's like some deathly game of dominoes: I can't really tell you about Abomination *because then I'd have to tell you about the disability, and I can't talk about that yet and so I can't tell you about the legal case.*

Or everything falls down.

They sat in silence.

Theo watched a group of students at a table across the room.

"*Don't* look right now," he said carefully, "in fact I will *murder* you if you look right now, but table by the door. Girl in the khaki coat. Ten o'clock. That's Lauren." Sophie nodded, sat a few minutes, then turned and rummaged in her backpack, one eye on the table.

"Ah. She's pretty." Sophie straightened up and ran a hand through her hair.

"She's *gorgeous*. And I hate her."

"Well, I hate her too, then. Still hurts?"

"Whatever. It's done. It makes you kind of cynical, though, you know? Closed. Less trusting." Theo shook his head.

Sophie, who'd learned early never to trust anybody, nodded, pretending she understood.

"How's stuff at home? It's not Calvin's fault that Lauren liked him, right?"

"Guess not. No. But we barely talk anymore. We never did, much. But now, nada. I used to think Calvin was such a great guy. You know, big brother hero worship bullshit. But he's not. Talk about a narcississist." Sophie let that one go. "But I'll let you in on a little secret," he continued, "he's cheating on Tamara."

"No! *Theo!*"

"*Yes.* I don't know her name, but the girl came to our door all crying and needing to see Calvin, who was out. So, Mom got the whole story from her and *boom!*" Theo mimed a massive explosion, eyes wide, hands shaping it. "When Calvin came home ..." Theo shook his head and grimaced. "Ug-ul-y. Lots and lotsa fighting. I'm staying out of the house. I'm basically just sleeping there at this point. Like a hostel."

"Well, come over to my house any time you want." She was annoyed she felt uncomfortable inviting her closest friend over.

"Thanks, Ronny. Not too comfortable with that one, though. I mean, your parents *scare* me, and your gran just died and everything."

Oh, Theo. My "gran" just dying is truly the very least of all of our miserable troubles.

She couldn't figure out a way to tell Theo about her disease. Disability. She couldn't. It felt way too private, still too cold and too terrifying to put into words. Plus, there never, ever seemed to be a good time. You don't launch into a description of your life-shortening disease over a mochaccino, the inevitable loss of emotion, movement, and thought over takeout pizza. Do you? She was new to this. She would tell him when she was ready. It was her call. She didn't owe anybody anything. Not even Theo.

"Well, I'm not sleeping well lately," *basically at all*, "so if you ever want to talk, any time, call me. I'm probably up."

"Thanks, Ronny. You're the best. Hey, only two weeks until summer vacation. Do you, uh, have exams and everything in that class you're in?"

"Just Legal Studies. You?"

"Yeah, four exams. Then freedom. Wait, did I say *freedom*? I meant work. I guess I'll go back to the car wash, which I hated last summer. But now that I've known the staggering joy of working at Parthenon, the car wash is looking okay. And there's not much else out there. God. Isn't being young supposed to be fun? Ever? *You* don't have to work, I bet. What're you going to do?"

Probably just freak out alone in my room about how little life I have left, Theo. It'll be a total party.

"Not sure yet. I should probably make a list or something."

Chapter Twenty-Seven

HER BEDROOM CLOCK SAID 3:47 a.m. Sophie was making a list: *List of Things to Do With the Rest of My Life.*

The binder of university admissions pamphlets that she'd been collecting since she was in middle school sat shoved into her garbage can. She felt about a hundred years old thinking about how she used to leaf through the binder, imagining herself as a stylish college student, lounging on the pristine lawn of one of the Ivy Leagues. Her father had wanted her to try for Oxford, her mother had argued for Columbia. All of it useless, meaningless now. Four years. She could do something other than cram for exams for four years. Plus, her doctors, her therapists were here.

It's starting already. It's altering my life …

She'd always known she never wanted to be a lawyer or an English professor. She'd seen too much of those careers. Too much, and too up close. All the petty jealousies of English departments and law firms, the bickering, the infighting. She was a good writer, she knew that, and had a pseudonym (R.S. John) ready in case she ever wrote anything worth publishing. She dreaded the idea of people finding out she was Mariam's granddaughter, though. Her latest plan had been to become a teacher. She was good with kids, she loved kids.

God, *children*. She had also assumed that, someday, she'd have kids. The problem was that until now, she imagined events unfolding gradually in her life. Her senior year. Maybe a trip after high school graduation. Upgrading her marks, going away to university. Maybe an exchange or volunteering overseas. Some sort of satisfying career, a place of her own. A few boyfriends, hopefully, or maybe just one special one. A long-term relation- ship. Kids. Growing old.

None of that was realistic, now. Especially the "growing old" part. She thought of Mariam, lying under the covers, the skunk- streak of white hair down her part. *I won't ever get gray hair,* she realized with a paralyzing shock. *I won't have a face full of wrin- kles, a homemade card or a hug from a grandchild.*

I would have been a good grandma, a good mother, she thought with immense sadness.

It was ludicrous to even think about having a child, ridicu- lous, irresponsible, even negligent. There was a dangerous 50% chance of passing on this disease. Who would gamble on that? Never mind that she'd never had a boyfriend, never even really kissed or been kissed. That disgusting tongue-slide of Tyler Bauer at that grade seven dance didn't count.

So much of what we plan isn't even important, she realized. She was officially middle-aged, maybe even old in Huntington Disease dog years. It was a flat-out race against time. No time to think about what to *be*. No time to be qualified for anything, and no point either. School seemed like a huge, criminal waste of the time she had left.

What, then? What was left? Sitting around this house she hated, worrying about her body's every tick and twitch, freaking about every forgotten word or meltdown or stumble? Going on

an endless round of appointments with doctors and physiotherapists and social workers? Watching Mom and Dad watching her?
Not really living, just existing, just maintaining this body, for as
long as she could? Just staving off non-being? What on earth was
the point of that?

She jumped up and flung open the window. The breeze wafted
in, fresh and fragrant. Trees dark against an indigo sky punched
with stars. The moon a gleaming half-pie. Silence, but not silence.
The rustle of leaves, the creak of a branch. And her clock: ticking, ticking, ticking. She grabbed it and flung it out into the yard,
smiled as she heard it crack against a tree and drop.

She was here, now. Now, right now, she was alive. Not like
Mariam, wherever Mariam was. Mariam had grabbed what she
wanted in the selfish, long life she'd had. She needed to stop
mourning the time she had left and take a hold of it, grab it, really
live it. Harness that primitive part of her, the streak that snatched
what it wanted in its sharp teeth and gobbled it whole.

Live what was left of her life as she wanted. Fast. Intensely.
Meaningfully.

So, what did she want? She stared out into the night.

I want to be loved. I want to love. Those were easy; she'd craved
those her whole life.

I want to travel, to see something of the world.

I want to really live.

A list of sorts formed in her mind, as she looked up at the
stars. It wasn't the sort of list she'd imagined, tied as it was to desperate urgency and action. But it became clearer. Stark.

If she wanted love, she had to find it quickly.

If she wanted to travel, she should go as soon as possible.

If she wanted to really live, she should figure out how.

Chapter Twenty-Eight

"ANY EXPLANATION FOR THIS?" HER father swiveled his laptop around. Another article about Mariam.

"What is it?" Sophie barely looked up from spreading peanut butter on toast.

"It's *The Rover*. Apparently, they asked you for a comment on your grandmother's passing, and you told them to, and I quote, 'go f-word yourselves.'"

"I said 'fuck,' so — not accurate. And they claim to be a reputable news outlet."

"Very funny. Honestly, Sophie, *dignity*! How many times have your mother and I told you to say, 'no comment'? We really don't need this kind of bad press."

"What do I care, Dad? What do *you* even care?"

"I *care*, because it is Mariam's reputation, and by association *our* reputation that's at stake."

Sophie shrugged, picked up her plate, and turned to go to her room.

He called after her angrily. "Don't walk away! I *care* because the eyes of the world are upon us."

"Oh, God, just listen to yourself, Dad." She turned wearily. "'*The eyes of the world.*' Seriously? What are you, Winston Churchill?"

"It happens to be the truth. So, if you can't behave —"

"— like the simpering, devoted, awestruck, grateful little granddaughter I'm supposed to be, then what, Dad? What?"

"Then you won't be coming to the ... to the ..."

"Funeral?" She nearly laughed. "You're grounding me from Mariam's funeral? I'm crushed, Dad. *Crushed*. Because I was so looking *forward* to the funeral. Of being reminded of death yet again."

They looked at each other bleakly, then both looked away.

"I'm sorry," her father said, looking down at his hands, "I know this is a difficult time for you."

"Look, Dad, I'll put on an act tomorrow at the funeral. But that 'celebration of life' Mariam's publisher is planning in New York? That ... that ... Mariampalooza?"

Her father gave an unexpected snort of laughter.

"I'm not coming to that," Sophie said. "No *way*."

She saw guilty relief in his eyes.

"Relieved?" she said before she could stop herself.

"A little," he said, again unexpectedly. *Laughter, honesty, a shred of sympathy ... what next?* Sophie thought. "But if you stay, you'll have to be civil to any reporters. Just civil."

"Gotcha. No f-bombs. Oh, and I'll be fine, Dad, all by myself, so stop worrying about me already," she said sarcastically, taking a bite of toast.

"We'll only be gone a couple of days. You could invite a friend to stay with you, that Fiona from school or someone." *Name another friend of mine, Dad. Do you even know Theo's name?* "I'll ask Harriet and Ron from next door to look in."

"Don't you dare. Harriet's already desperate for all the gory, death-porn details of Mariam's death."

"Don't be crude. Anyway, you can just tell any reporters —"

"— to go fuck themselves. Got it." Again, she was surprised by her father's bark of laughter. "Just kidding, Dad. I'll behave."

"Thank you," he said. Then he sighed. "Your mother and I are also in the process of negotiating the contract for your mother's biography of Mariam. And control over her papers, her reputation, her legacy. The estate, her works in progress, settling outstanding accounts. It's all a bit of a mess, legally speaking." He closed his eyes and rubbed a shaky hand on his forehead.

Sophie watched him. He looked old, tired.

"Dad, you gotta take care of yourself in all this."

"Why wouldn't she have left a will?" he asked, baffled. "Just a scrawled 'everything to my daughter,' properly witnessed. How many times did I tell her? Elisabeth was her only daughter, there were no ties left to any of the husbands. It could have been so simple, instead of which she leaves a complete nightmare."

"Well, that's probably why, Dad. Given the choice, Mariam would always have picked the nightmare."

In the days following Mariam's death, Sophie despised herself for wondering if Mariam might have actually left something, anything, for her. It didn't matter what it was. A paperweight. A pair of earrings. A fricking paper clip. Anything left to her specifically, anything to show she'd possibly mattered a little to her. There had been nothing. Nothing for Sophie or her mother. No family heirloom passed down, no object invested with sentimental value. Mariam was as selfish in death as she had been in life.

"I have a will," her father said loudly, then cleared his throat.

"Okay," Sophie eyed him warily.

"Everything to your mother if I predecease her, which appears highly likely," he swallowed, "and she has a will leaving everything to you. If we die simultaneously, for instance in a plane or a car crash," he seemed soothed by these legal contingencies, "you inherit everything. Come to think of it, *you* should —" He stopped.

"I should what?" No answer. "I should *what*, Dad? Make a *will*? That's ridiculous." Her voice choked on the word, her eyes blurred with tears.

"It's sensible. A good sum of money involved."

"Sure, Dad, I'll get right on that. I'll use that fancy pen," she tossed over her shoulder as she left the room.

Not ridiculous. Not even remotely ridiculous. It's one more thing to add to the list.

Chapter Twenty-Nine

SOPHIE SAT IN THE HARD pew in the hot, crowded church. She wriggled surreptitiously to ease the irritation of the nylons on her inner thighs and watched the people lining up to pay their last respects. It was an open casket, Mariam looking like a wax figure, a store-window mannequin, looking nothing like Mariam had ever looked. Someone, and Sophie couldn't imagine who could tolerate such a grotesque job, had touched up Mariam's roots, blushed up her normally sallow cheeks and applied lipstick (which she never wore). Sophie gave a little shudder of revulsion at strangers touching Mariam's lifeless body, manhandling her into clothes, putting makeup on her face, and displaying her like a macabre doll for other people to gawk at.

Why do we do these things? Mental note: tell someone I want to be cremated. Or parts of me donated — eyes and organs, whatever they need. Do they do teeth? — and the rest of me burned. She gave herself a sharp pinch. *Stop it.*

The sun streamed in through the stained-glass windows, and the scent of lilies and old incense was suffocating. People packed into the pews, lined the walls, stood at the back of the church, and filled the overflow rooms. Who were they all? Sophie recognized almost nobody.

Did Mariam ever say she wanted a church funeral? Had she ever actually been to church? Sophie didn't know. Her mother and father weren't religious at all, and she assumed Mariam hadn't been either. Would she have wanted this train of admirers, mourners, and strangers staring at her? It seemed indecent to Sophie, it seemed like nothing Mariam could ever have borne. But who knows? Maybe vanity would have outweighed fastidiousness, and she'd have seen all this as a fitting tribute.

Mariam hadn't, it seems, ever talked to her daughter and son-in-law about her eventual death, her wishes, her preferences. Hadn't made a will, hadn't gotten her affairs in order, hadn't done a thing; it was as if she'd assumed she'd live forever, until she decided not to.

So, Sophie's parents improvised and followed the script laid out by society and funeral directors and put on the whole show: an expensive coffin, enormous bouquets of flowers, the best hors d'oeuvres money could buy. Reputations at stake — hers and theirs.

Sophie's head pounded rhythmically along with the mournful organ music. A trickle of sweat slid down the side of her face. Her black dress, bought in a rush, was itchy and tight across the shoulders; her feet, wedged into new, excruciating kitten heels were throbbing. She vowed to herself to never wear nylons again.

The priest or minister or whatever he was began the ceremony. Up and down, up and down — everyone in the church but her family seemed to know the drill of when to stand and when to sit. Sophie sat through it all, not trusting her shaky legs and her pounding head.

"Sophie, *up*," hissed her mother the first time. But when she saw Sophie's face, she said, "Never mind. Just sit."

Her parents left the pew to perform an awkward joint eulogy. Sophie winced as her father stumbled and very nearly fell up the three steps to the microphone, her mother using all her strength to steady him. They looked, Sophie thought, like a couple who'd had way too much to drink. Her mother had the dazed, careful look of someone on heavy medication.

"Who left those steps there?" Her father got the joke in quickly and had the audience chuckling. He must have had years of addressing his symptoms head-on like that, Sophie realized, diffusing accidents with humor, getting in the shot at himself before somebody else did. Those five words gave her a brief glimpse into her father's life.

He was an engaging public speaker, Sophie realized, even if his fake accent did get more pronounced. Her mother, who spoke in front of classes daily, was pinched and nervous, and came across as dry, pompous, and humorless. She began by listing Mariam's many awards and achievements. Winner of the Pulitzer, shortlisted for the Booker Prize, on and on. As though those were the important things, as though those dry titles actually mattered in a life.

Sophie's mother read from her paper, quoting and using literary allusions, blinking up occasionally, like some academic at a useless conference. She called Mariam *Mariam,* never *Mother* or *Mom.* Sophie was glad she wasn't faking that.

She looked down at her twitching hands. Her head had begun to swim, and she felt panic claw at her stomach. She tried closing her eyes, taking some long, deep breaths to calm herself. She gripped her hands together hard, trying to focus on anything but the panic slicing through her. *I will not have a seizure here. I will not black out. I will not disgrace myself and have everyone think-ing that I'm prostrated with grief because Mariam is gone.* But the blackness in her head closed in, and she crouched over her knees as far as her dress allowed.

What was she even doing here among all these strangers, in these unfamiliar clothes, participating in this celebration of a woman who'd only ever been cruel? Wasting precious minutes of her precious life. The utter meaninglessness of it, and the enor-mity of her isolation washed over her, and she drew a shuddering breath; how alone can a person feel before they actually disap-pear? She was slipping away, floating, like a lost balloon.

A hand touched her back.

"You okay, Ronny?"

She turned her head to see Theo's anxious face down near hers. Theo's dear, familiar face, his touch pulling her back to the world.

"Ronny, you okay? You look … lost."

He was dressed in unfamiliar clothes. Dress shirt and pants. Tie. Dress shoes that looked a bit big. Maybe his dad's or Calvin's.

"Theo," she whispered. "You look nice. I'm trying not to faint or throw up."

"Excellent, that's good. You keep on trying." He held her hot hand in his cool, dry one. "Just take it easy. Here." He grabbed the funeral program from the pew and fanned it near her face. "You want me to get you some water? I got time; your mom and dad are still droning on up there. I saw you kind of crumple there, and I know this row is reserved for family, but I thought, *screw it, I gotta go help poor Ronny.*"

Sophie blinked away hot tears. Nobody had ever been so kind to her in her whole life.

"Where have you been sitting?" she murmured.

"Scrum at the back. Standing."

"It was nice of you to come." *Nice.* What an inadequate word.

"Hella hot in here," he muttered, fanning both of them, "and your folks just keep on wanting to talk and talk up there. They got a *whole* lot to say about your granny."

Sophie sat up and brushed her hair back from her face.

"You look a little less deathlike," Theo whispered encouragingly.

"Bet you say that to all the girls," Sophie said. Both of them shuddered with silent giggles. Church-giggles. Stress-giggles. Getting them under control, then looking at each other, then losing it again.

Her parents were bringing the eulogy to a close. "And Mariam, living true to her own words from her seminal novel, *Abomination*, has gone away, away, *her* way, into the gathering night."

"Can't get away from that story, hey?" Theo whispered. "Remember: *Monstrosity.* Solid gold. Get on it. They're heading back; I better go." He squeezed her hand and slid out of the pew. It took all her energy not to follow him.

She turned and stared after him as he walked quickly down the side of the church, head held high, until he disappeared into the crowd at the back.

You didn't have to come to this, Theo. But you came.

Not for Mariam, not for my parents.

For me.

"JUST 'NO COMMENT' TO REPORTERS, please, Sophie," her mother said crisply as they came back from watching Mariam's shiny black coffin lowered into a deep, dark pit in the ground.

After which they, bizarrely and somehow weirdly aggressively, threw dirt down on top of it. *Take that, Mariam! Take that!*

The whole thing was surreal, movie-like.

"And just *polite* to everyone else. Cordial. 'Thank you for coming,' that kind of thing."

It was warm, the sun streaming through the trees, but at least there was a gentle breeze. The old graveyard seemed a peaceful place. Too peaceful for Mariam, but maybe her wax body wouldn't stir up the trouble it did when it was alive. Why here? Sophie wondered. Mariam had, she supposed, lived here off and on for a bit of her life. But when Sophie thought of Mariam, she never thought of her sedentary, in one place.

"A nomad, a gypsy," was how Mariam had glorified her restlessness.

Well, Mariam, you're pretty much parked here for good, now.

"Thank you for coming." Sophie smiled and shook hands with strangers. Writers and students and lawyers and neighbors and friends of her parents, everyone wanting to say how a*ma*zing Mariam had been, how irre*place*able. People like the Dean of the English department who held Sophie's hand too long and pulled her in uncomfortably close while she told her some long Mariam story, Sophie reeling from her heavy, revolting perfume. Sleek lawyers in expensive suits who came in packs. Sophie's mother's English students shaking her hand while looking past her for more important people. Mariam's agent, spiky gray hair and sharp pale-blue eyes behind heavy glasses. People like Mariam's former husband (number three? number five?), who shook Sophie's hand with both of his, looked genuinely shaken and said this world wasn't big enough for the likes of Mariam Gayle. Sophie wondered how he had survived

Mariam. She could just hear Mariam's sneer: *He was always ridiculously sentimental.*

People kept coming at her until her back ached from standing, until her feet in their tight shoes seemed to develop pulses of their own. Her smile felt like more of a grimace, like she was actively baring her teeth at people. She stopped even thanking them for coming and just held out her hand and let them talk. Sometimes it was like turning on a tap — they'd waited their turn, they'd stocked up things to say and now here they were with the family, and gush, gush, gush. They had an autographed copy of blank, they met Mariam at the book launch for blank, they saw blank star in the West End production of blank, they were transported hearing Mariam doing a reading from blank, blank was their favorite movie adaptation of all time.

And all the time she wondered where Theo was.

Sophie bore it as long as she could, until she was white-faced and exhausted, shaky and numb. Then she excused herself and hid in a bathroom stall for half an hour. Finally, she crept out, filled a plate with food, and took it to a quiet corner. She pulled out her phone.

lots of good food here, Theo.

want to come back?

Chapter Thirty

THE DAY AFTER THE FUNERAL, the day before her parents were
leaving for New York and the publisher's reception (*Mariam Gayle:
Life, Literature, Legend*), Sophie's parents were still fuming about
the incident near the end of the funeral reception. Her father had
introduced her to yet another meaningless person, a small man
with abundant white hair. She hadn't caught the name, merely stood
up, shook his hand, and gave her dutiful, teeth-baring grimace.

"How's the air up there?" the man asked, pretending to be
amazed by her immense height. "*Well.* You certainly didn't take
after your petite grandmother."

"Ahaha." Her father had laughed with the man. Laughed at
her. "No. No, she did *not.*" He shot a warning glance at Sophie's
stony face.

"Don't worry, don't worry," — the man patted her shoulder
comfortingly — "there's plenty of tall young men out there that
might like a big girl."

This was where, she realized, she was supposed to keep smiling and put up with any other assorted insults he chose to lob her
way. Nope. Life really *was* too short.

"What about *your* grandmother," she said, as though she was
really interested. She bent down with her hands on her knees like
someone talking to a toddler. "Was she a little shrimp like *you*?"

Her father hurriedly pulled the man away, talking loudly about how Sophie was exhausted, prostrated with grief, on medication, a teenager, acting out, hormonal, not herself. Later, after a tense drive home, after her father had slammed out of the car, her mother turned to her. White face, pinched nose, mouth thinned in anger.

"That man to whom you were inexcusably rude was the *Minister of Culture*."

"So? So what? He was rude to me first," Sophie said. "Did Dad tell you what he said to *me*?"

"He was our *guest*. An important guest. At Mariam's *funeral*."

There was no arguing. There never had been. Sophie tried to remember if they had ever taken her side. All she remembered was them siding with the merest acquaintance, the casual dinner guest, the visiting dignitary, the dead grandmother.

She was trying to love them, but they were making it hard.

SOPHIE REALIZED SHE HAD TO act soon on something that had until yesterday been just an idea.

I have to ask now, today. While they're exhausted from the funeral, wary of my outbursts, uncertain about how I'm feeling. Now, while they're busy, thinking of the memorial hoopla in New York, leaving tomorrow.

And there was no time to feel guilty for being cynical about it. *That's how this family operates.*

Late afternoon, and she found her father sitting in the basement. It was odd to find him in a completely unfinished part of the house; he only ever attempted the rickety steps to snatch a bottle of wine for a dinner party. But there he was, sitting in one of the ancient chairs on the carpet remnant, flipping through old photo albums.

He looked up warily.

"Dad, I'm sorry I was rude to that man. The government guy."

"The Minister of Culture."

"Yes, well, even though he was rude to me first —"

"He was *joking!*"

"He was *hurtful.* Jokes can be cruel, you know. Still, I'm sorry I called him a shrimp. Mostly I'm sorry I embarrassed you and Mom. I was exhausted. Sick. Totally overwhelmed. But I'm sorry. I know it wasn't exactly a picnic for you and Mom."

Her father sighed.

"All right. It's done. I think I smoothed things over with him. He's establishing a literary award in Mariam's name."

"Nice," Sophie said, hoping she didn't sound as fake as she felt. "Well, again. Sorry."

There was a silence.

"Sick, how?" her father said, glancing up sharply. "You were feeling sick?"

"Not that," she said flatly. "It was just so hot, and I felt a bit faint. Lurchy."

He cleared his throat.

"I find, with the lurchy bits, that it often helps to take smaller, more controlled steps."

"Ah," Sophie said, shying away from swapping infirmity tips, but touched that her father was trying. "Good, I'll try that. Thanks."

She picked up a photo album and flipped through it. An old one. Her mother had long hair; her father had more hair.

"You guys looked good! All ... groovy, man. What are you doing down here?"

"Well, they'll have loads of *official* pictures of Mariam for the memorial," he said. "News clips. Author pics. I just thought I'd find something a little more personal. A family shot, or something casual, a side of Mariam people haven't seen before. For our speech."

Trying to find a picture of Mariam with her family might be a challenge, Sophie thought. *Also, good luck finding one where she's not openly loathing us.*

"Good idea. You two knew her better than anybody."

"I don't know about that. She was rarely here. Always traveling."

Perfect opening.

"Look, can I talk to you about something?"

He sat back, looking slightly wary.

"Of course."

"I need your advice."

He raised his eyebrows. *Not what he'd been expecting,* she thought.

"Well, I think we all need a break from each other. I know I've been difficult. I can't seem to help it. We haven't talked about this disease we both have, but we have to face facts sometime. My life isn't what I thought it was going to be. It'll be much ... shorter." Her voice thickened unexpectedly over that last, damning word.

"Do we really need to talk about this now?" Alarm quickened in her father's voice. He pitched the album he was holding into an open box. "Dr. Strickland is a far better resource —"

"Yes, we need to. I need to start *living*, Dad. Doing some of the things I need to do. With my *life.*" She took a deep breath. "I want to use some of the money from the court case to travel. Not a ton, just a bit. To go away for a little while. A few weeks, a month, maybe. I have a friend who might come with me. Probably would come with me. Have adventures, be young, carefree. You always talk about that backpacking trip you took in Europe after you graduated high school."

"I *just* looked at those photos, actually," her father said, smiling. She pounced at the box.

"Which, this one?" She flipped open an album. "You were so *young*. Where is this?" She pointed to a random picture of her father and his friend.

"Ah, let's see. Spain, I think. Spain, Portugal, and Italy," he said. "Biking around Europe. Hosteling. Marty and I had such a great time: soaked in the rain, baked by the sun, *adventure*."

"So, it was worth going, right?"

"It was one of the happiest trips of my life."

"Well, *I* want an amazing trip, Dad! Can't you see? And I don't have a lot of time to work with. I want to do a trip, now, soon, this summer, while I'm still … me."

Her father was silent for a long time, looking down. She noticed the tremors in his clasped hands before he tucked them tight between his knees.

She opened her mouth and shut it again.

Don't rush him, Sophie. Let him think.

When he finally looked up, his face was a complicated mix of emotions. She saw relief. Resignation. Exhaustion. Sympathy. And a glimpse of fear.

"Great plan. How much do you need?"

Chapter Thirty-One

THE PLANE'S ENGINE ROARED INTO serious, I-mean-business take-off mode and it began to hurtle down the final runway.

"I love this part," said Theo, peering past her to look at the lights speeding by. "All the waiting, the inching away from the gate, the turning onto the runway, all that piddly shit is *over*. Engine's roaring, and we are *storming* this runway!"

"We're really doing this, Theo," Sophie said, studying the side of his face. "Backpacking. Europe!" *And maybe changing our tickets, staying longer, coming back through Asia,* she thought. She'd wait for the right time to suggest that.

"Actually *doing* it, Ronny," he said, bumping his fist on her thigh excitedly. "Unreal."

Theo had taken some convincing. A *lot* of convincing. The sticking point was the money, the thought that her parents were paying for the trip.

"I do have some tiny, tattered bits of pride left, Ronny," he'd said. "Your folks don't want to pay for some guy they don't even know, and I don't want them to, either."

"It's actually *my money*, Theo," she had finally yelled at him. "Understand? Mine. In trust, for *me*! Long story, and I will tell you sometime. But just stop being an idiot. We can go, get out there instead of just talking about it all the time. Celebrate our birthdays in *Paris*! Be young and free, remember?" She'd been terrified he'd say no, because she knew she wouldn't go on her own. Finally, finally, she wore him down with a barrage of photo texts. Pictures of the Mediterranean. A café in Paris. Berlin's Brandenburg Gate. Barcelona.

> how about the actual, fucking Parthenon instead of
> Parthenon Greek Eats?

ahahahahaha!
yeah, let's go.

"Okay, Ronny," he'd said, slapping money down on the Silvas' kitchen table. "$376 is what I got. Take it, but the rest of the trip is a *loan*. A short-term *loan*."

"Theo," she protested, but he talked over her, holding up a little notepad.

"See this? I'm going to keep track of everything. Every baguette, every glass of wine, every cup of coffee. Every chocolate. Every single frickin' euro and whatever they call the smaller change. And I'm paying you back half, okay?"

"Wow, that sounds *fun*," she'd said sarcastically. But her heart was singing, singing, singing.

"See it from my perspective, Ronny. That's probably money for your university or something. Would you seriously just take all that from me if things were reversed?"

"I would take it and *run*," she'd laughed. "Okay, okay. Just kidding. We'll split everything fifty-fifty." Lie. But she'd leave that for another day.

Her parents had insisted on having Theo for dinner before

they left, "just to get to know him a little better." Her mother made a couple of Indian vegetarian dishes and basmati rice when she told her that Theo was a vegetarian. Her father brought home a cake from the bakery near the firm. Sophie was touched at these thoughtful small gestures, but worried about what they would all talk about. She dreaded her parents grilling Theo about his career plans; she couldn't remember them ever talking to someone her age.

"Prepare for the worst evening you've ever spent anywhere," she'd warned him nervously. "Like, the shittiest date ever." She was surprised at how much she wanted it to go well.

Theo came, nervous but prepared. Collared shirt. He asked her mother to recommend a Dickens novel to him, and she smiled when he said, "maybe a *thin* one to start off with. Guy wrote a *lot*, right? And maybe nothing too depressing. I mean *Bleak House*; right there in the title." Her mother laughed delightedly. Sophie felt envious at how easily her mother and Theo chatted, her mother rummaging through the bookshelves, pressing *Oliver Twist* on Theo ("a gift! I have *so* many copies"). Then he trailed after her father, listening to the home renovation saga, seeming to be genuinely interested.

"You are such a suck-up," she hissed at one point.

"Grow up, Ronny," he said with dignity. "I'm *adulting* here. Trying to absorb a little culture. I never knew this house is almost a hundred years old. I actually think that shit is cool. I kind of like your weird folks. They know I'm paying half of everything for the trip, right?"

And maybe, maybe I'll tell you about the money in Europe, Theo. Maybe I'll tell you everything. But now, right now, all I want to do is have you here, sitting beside me on this plane. I don't care that this flight is packed, that there's a baby screaming, that the flight attendant was snotty about the size of my carry-on, that we'll be crossing a deep, shark-infested, inky ocean at night. I don't care about any of it. I only care about you and me. My entire world right now: shrunk to two regulation-size, economy airplane seats.

Theo settled back in his seat, leaning his shoulder into hers as the plane roared down the runway.

"Wait for it … It's coming! That incredible *rush* when we lift off. I love that. *Hoo-hoo!* Ronny! Europe!"

She snatched his hand as the plane lifted off, a tear sliding down the side of her face.

He squeezed back, reassuring her, thinking she was scared.

They hurtled up, up, up, away from it all, into the gathering night.

Ever After

I'M WRITING TO YOU NOW, so you have a record of me. Of us.

I thought I would start this journal later, when you're actually born, but it has to be now. Today. This morning. It is October 24th, 2019. 9:30 a.m. Note that this is written in pen.

The test is today, and I want you to know now, beforehand, that the result will make no difference to us.

You're loved and wanted exactly as you are.

THE DOCTOR SAID "NORMAL!" TRIUMPHANTLY, as though she'd tinkered with your genes herself and engineered the result. It never mattered to me what your genes said but I had to know. Do you understand that? Not ever, ever to get rid of you if you'd tested positive for this disease, but to prepare. Just to prepare.

Anyway, I gave the doctor the fist bump she was expecting.

I promise to be honest with you here. I want you to have the truth I never had. So, the truth is that I am relieved. You had a 50-50 chance of inheriting this disease, and you fell on the safe side. I would have felt so guilty if you'd been unlucky. But I also feel guilty for saying that, guilty for feeling relief. But I can't honestly say I would have chosen my kind of life for you. What if you'd tested positive? How would I have felt? Gutted? Angry? I don't know. I honestly don't know. That seems a betrayal of everything — of myself, of my dad, of all the people I've met with this disease. Of every single person with a disability.

I would have kept you, loved you, and cherished you no matter what. I do know that.

But would you have hated me when you were old enough to know? Would you have thought I was selfish for wanting you? I hope not. Because life, any life, no matter how short, can have moments of such intense sweetness that who can say what is and is not worthy? Or wrongful? As Cutcheon J. (that old bastard; more on him later) took credit for his student saying: "who can measure the joy and love a child brings to its parents?" Who can measure what another person feels about their life?

Anyway, you're, as the good doctor says, "normal." Fist bump! You will never have to fear dependence on others, loss of yourself, a shortened life. I hope you won't ever fear for anything, but that's hoping too much. You won't have my problems; you'll have ones of your own. I hope they're small ones.

But you will have one thing I won't. Even though it hurts to write this, hurts to even think it: you can grow old with your dad, Little Bean. He calls you *Little Bean*. I wonder if he'll ever stop calling you that.

It seems strange thinking of Theo as a father. I know he felt strange for a long while there. Long after I told him I was pregnant, after the total shock and stress of it settled, he was mostly just amazed ("we built a baby. An actual baby? How'd two goofs like us even figure that out?"). And now he's really getting into it: getting me to call him Dad, Daddy, Father, and Pa to see how each "feels," calling me *wifey* (which, God help me, I love, even though it's technically not true. Yet.), talking about thrifting some "Dad clothes." He researches everything about you, obsessively. Today he said: "An avocado, Ronny! At sixteen weeks, Little Bean is as big as an avocado!" You've made us even closer. And me? I felt almost guilty to be absolutely thrilled from the start. Right from the shock! You've given me another person to live for.

Poor Theo. He didn't know what he was getting into with that trip to Europe. He didn't know how ferociously I wanted to start living, how I wanted everything now, now, now. Early in the trip, I blurted everything out to him. It was on a train from Paris to Marseilles, and somehow, I couldn't keep it in any longer. I didn't want there to be any secrets between us. I told him all about the disease, the court case, my parents, everything.

He pulled me into a long hug, such a long hug, and I remember both of us crying. Theo so quiet, for once speechless. But when we pulled into Marseilles, he said, "Starting now, Ronny, we are gonna LIVE."

It never happens how you think it will, the falling in love thing. Or at least it didn't for me.

I'd seen every side of your dad, my Theo. We've known each other since we were eight. Eight! I've seen the teeth he hadn't grown into yet; he saw mine before braces. I've seen him cry. I've seen him wreck a pair of pants crawling under a shed to see if a mangy stray cat was okay. I've seen him in a hairnet, in a ridiculously unflattering leather jacket (maroon; it was seventh grade) and also a jean vest (?!), swilling out car wash stalls with a squeegee. I've seen him adjust his friend Quinn's wig before his drag act for the talent show and help him up on stage because those platform shoes were insanely high. I've seen him, the least violent guy in the whole world, menace the bully who'd made his little brother's life hell for half a year. Honest to God, Little Bean, I've seen him in a horse-drawn carriage (long story, but he waved like the Queen).

And he's seen me. I shudder to think what he's seen. The terrible hair experiments, the lip piercing, so many dire fashion choices that I can't even begin to list them all. Okay, one: headband. No, two: crop top. He's suffered me pompously quoting poetry. He's seen me bitter and jealous and drunk. But he remembers good things, too. He told me, in one of our marathon conversations in Europe, that he remembers me sleeping over with Daria when her friends' parents were divorcing, and she had a lot of anxiety. He remembers me "galumphing" (a word I take exception to) down the street with a shrieking Crystal on my back, "and Ronny," he said, "not many people have time for that grim little kid." He remembers always loving the sound of my laugh, being able to make me laugh, how serious and absorbed I look when I'm writing or reading. He thinks I have the most "amazing" eyes he's ever seen. You have no idea how I've stored up these things and think of them on bleak days.

I knew I loved him at your great-grandmother's funeral. Wouldn't have chosen that as the place or the time to fall in love, but I remember the exact minute. He slipped into the pew when my parents were giving that wretched tribute to Mariam, and I was exhausted and hot and blacking out and generally at the level of rock-bottom despair. He touched my back, fanned my face, asked if I was feeling all right. I looked over at him (we were both hunched over at the time), and it was all there, it was like coming home after being out in the cold, into a real home with warmth and love. No glamour at all. Just rock-solid rightness. Brightness. When he walked away — I can still see him in my head — jaunty stride, broad shoulders, thin body, head held high, he was so far superior to anyone else there, so much kinder, nobler. He was my family.

He'd come there for me, only for me. That still seems incredible. Nobody seemed to have ever really cared about me before unless, like Mom and Dad, they kind of had to (I like to think I've sort of grown on them). But he saw something lovable in me. And in a flash, I saw that it was him that I loved, had loved for a long, long time. Not the glamorous somebody (long story, but your dad is worth about a hundred glamorous somebodies) I once thought I cared for. It was your dad who saved my life.

Telling Theo about my altered life totally changed things between us. The shock of it, the seriousness of it, the bigness of it clarified immediately for both of us what was important. It was like everything else dropped away, leaving only us standing there together. There was this shared sense of urgency, a delight in each moment, a closeness like neither of us had ever felt.

Europe seemed at first like the goal, but it became the backdrop. The world revolved around us. And we laughed and did stupid shit (ask him some time about the balcony and the melon) and wandered and ran and waded into fountains and rode buses just to see where they ended up.

It was in Athens one special day that everything electrified; wandering around the real Parthenon, I told him that I thought I'd been in love with him most of my life. He stopped right in the middle of a German tourist's picture and had me repeat that. Somewhere in, like, Munich, there's a picture of Theo looking shocked against the backdrop of the Parthenon. He needed a lot of convincing that Calvin was nothing to me; I needed a lot of convincing when he said he'd have asked me out a long time ago if he'd known he had a chance. This precious thing: there for both of us all along, and we'd been too stupid or scared to grab it.

That strange, wonderful day. We couldn't find a place to stay anywhere, neither of us being even remotely organized and Athens being super crowded with some summer music festival. Finally, around midnight, a hostel owner told us we could camp up on hostel's roof. Just us, on this big, hard, flat roof. The view! Twinkling lights and dark hills and lapping ocean, like the whole world was spread out for us.

We made a nest of towels and clothes and backpacks and huddled together against the cold and talked and laughed and sang and listened to the tourists partying and fell deeper in love and stared up at the deep sky and the stars. And ... well, you're a kid, so maybe I'd better censor myself (I can't ever imagine wanting to hear about my parents being romantic). Anyway, it was the most perfect, most magical night of my life. I don't know if that's the night that created you, but I hope it was — in an ancient country, love given and returned, under the stars on a perfect, perfect night.

So, after six weeks of traveling through Europe and Asia, here we are, me and you and Theo.

I am going to fight with everything that is in me to spend as much time as I can with both of you. I will go to all the doctors and therapists; I will jump through any hoop they tell me to. I will never take a minute for granted. We might have ten years! That's still a long time, right? Ten years ago, I was seven. And ten years from now you'll be, like, nine years old! I remember being that age (I was clumsy and big and unhappy, but don't worry, not every nine-year-old is. Your dad is slim and semi-coordinated and very positive, so maybe you'll inherit those better things from him).

I will also try to forget the ticking of time. It is not the boss of me, or of you, or of any of us. Only one small part of life is measured by a clock.

Whatever happens, at least I'll have had years and years with you. At least you'll go on, without fears, without worries. And you'll have a wonderful father. Aunts and uncles! Really, really lovely grandparents on your dad's side. And on mine, a smart and healthy grandmother (who, by the way, will need a lot of loving and cheering up; she's had a hard life), and a kind and possibly not-so-healthy grandfather, both of whom I'm getting to know and appreciate much better. And a cat! You'll get to know Nick. He'll be a crabby old loaf of a cat, but cats can live until they're twenty or something, I think. Give him a scratch right where his tail meets his back. He loves that.

The doctors are trying their best. They have a treatment plan for me. My life on a spreadsheet. I appreciate that support so much. They recognize this disease in me, but like some wild animal, they're not quite sure how it'll behave. It's different for everyone. Will it lurk, hunker down warily, or will it pounce and snap? Or will it surprise us all?

But ultimately, the doctors only know a little part of me. They don't know that bright, strong, inner core of me, the one that refuses to admit defeat. The one that will fight for this happiness, this love, this home that I've found, as long as it possibly can. Nobody knows how much time they have. But the point isn't the amount; it's how you live the time you have.

And when my time comes, you just look up, Little Bean, and there I'll be — flying, with my face to the stars.

That got a little heavy. Sorry.

Your dad and I are moving to a little place of our own near the university so he can walk to his classes. First of the month! It's small, but who cares? Theo needs to get out of his house, and I want us to have a home of our own. One with love and laughter, and stupid jokes and secondhand, mismatching, cheap furniture and takeout eaten straight out of the containers. He only wants a non-lumpy bed and maybe a couple of drippy candles in those corny Chianti bottles. He's planning on building us a bookshelf. Not sure how that's going to go.

And I've made a will — everything to your dad and you. You're the first to know. Money seems so small, but I like to think about how that money, that seemed so terrible when I first discovered it, might make things easier for you and your dad/pa/father later.

And in April, we get to meet you! Hold you, touch you! It makes me breathless just thinking about you, about watching you sleep, watching you grow. I'm already helpless at the wonder of you. I can't imagine how it will be when we know each other so much better.

I stopped by Room 107 to see everyone. Grace isn't there anymore. Ms. Linden said she's being fostered by her aunt, but Ms. Linden is checking in regularly. Good old Ms. Linden: I want you to meet her. I met the two new students before Lucy and Wayne practically tackled me in a group hug when they got back from speech path, Adnan brightened up a little and flapped, and Fiona and I talked and laughed and fed Morton like old times. Maybe our family will get a fish like Morton, another little fighter. Anyway, I'll go back every so often, Ms. Linden made me promise. I would have anyway.

It seems incredible, Little Bean, that I once felt so alone. One time, when little Crystal was so sad about being excluded, I remember thinking: get used to it, my little friend, we're all alone. But the thing is, you don't have to be alone if you let others in. I must remember to tell her that the next time I see her out there kicking her fence.

Your mother is officially a high school dropout. I'd have had to go for two more years to get enough credits to graduate, and I have other things to think about. You, of course. And I'm working for Dr. Strickland part-time, helping to coordinate the support group for JHD, which involves some data entry but also lots of talking and talking and talking with people. Sad stories but really wonderful people. It's giving me strength.

I'm also writing again. A lot: this new project is just pouring out of me in urgent, free, exhilarating writing. I think it will be a novel. Working title: Life Expectancy.

Speaking of writing, this has turned out to be a way longer journal entry than I'd planned. Sorry. I'll stop soon.

So: to recap. You're perfect (even if you are an avocado). I'm not. And your father is weird, but in a very good way.

Last thing: I want to give you some advice. Because I assume a mother is supposed to give advice? Even if she doesn't know anything about anything, my guess is she's supposed to fake it. Two things are clear to me now. I know that numbers only tell part of a story; someone who only lives for forty years might live a fuller, more intense, more meaningful life than someone who lives for eighty. Your life is your own, Little Bean, and it's your life expectancy — what you expect of your very own precious life — that matters. It's yours to live. So really live.

And I know that no life is wrongful. Flawed, maybe. Wasted, sure. Wrongful in itself, right from the start? No. Never let anybody tell you otherwise.

And you, me, and your dad? We're all here, now, right now, this minute, living in this world together.

Isn't that incredible?

Isn't that almost unimaginably wonderful?

Isn't that enough?

Acknowledgments

I am grateful for the talented team at DCB who helped bring this novel to publication. Special thanks to Barry Jowett for his insightful editorial suggestions, and Jennifer Rabby for her beautiful cover illustration.

Thanks to my literary agent, Hilary McMahon, for her thoughtful comments and her advocacy for this novel, and the Canada Council for the Arts for helping to support its creation.

Finally, thanks to my family who has, for many years, listened patiently to me describe the meandering path of this story's development. I'm sure they are as relieved as I am that we've finally arrived.

About the Author

Alison Hughes is the award-winning author of twenty books for children and young adults. Her YA novel *Hit the Ground Running* was a finalist for the Governor General's Literary Awards. Hughes' works have also won the R. Ross Annett Award and the Writers' Union of Canada Writing for Children Award, and have been nominated for numerous provincial children's choice awards. Hughes is a university writing advisor and gives workshops and presentations at schools, libraries, conferences, and festivals. She lives in Edmonton, Alberta.

We acknowledge the sacred land on which Cormorant Books operates. It has been a site of human activity for 15,000 years. This land is the territory of the Huron-Wendat and Petun First Nations, the Seneca, and most recently, the Mississaugas of the Credit River. The territory was the subject of the Dish With One Spoon Wampum Belt Covenant, an agreement between the Iroquois Confederacy and Confederacy of the Ojibway and allied nations to peaceably share and steward the resources around the Great Lakes. Today, the meeting place of Toronto is still home to many Indigenous people from across Turtle Island. We are grateful to have the opportunity to work in the community, on this territory.

We are also mindful of broken covenants and the need to strive to make right with all our relations.